Someone was dead . . . but who?

"I never liked the girl! Was it her?"

"Is it Roberta? She was so depressed after Dale spoke."

"Was she pushed? Who wanted her dead?"

"I think she jumped."

"I knew something was wrong about this whole business. Roberta told me only yesterday . . ."

"Where's Lucy? Is it her down there?"

"Has anyone seen Susan? She and her mother were at odds lately . . ."

"I don't want to get mixed up in anything to do with the police."

"Roberta's parties are always disasters, but this is too much."

By Joyce Christmas
Published by Fawcett Books:

Lady Margaret Priam mysteries:
A FÊTE WORSE THAN DEATH
SUDDENLY IN HER SORBET
SIMPLY TO DIE FOR
A STUNNING WAY TO DIE
FRIEND OR FAUX
IT'S HER FUNERAL
A PERFECT DAY FOR DYING
MOURNING GLORIA
GOING OUT IN STYLE
DYING WELL

Betty Trenka mysteries:
THIS BUSINESS IS MURDER
DEATH AT FACE VALUE
DOWNSIZED TO DEATH
MOOD TO MURDER

DYING WELL

A Lady Margaret
Priam Mystery

Joyce Christmas

FAWCETT BOOKS • NEW YORK

A Fawcett Book
Published by The Ballantine Publishing Group
Copyright © 2000 by Joyce Christmas

Fawcett is a registered trademark and the Fawcett colophon is a trademark of Random House, Inc.

www.randomhouse.com/BB/

Library of Congress Catalog Card Number: 99-91872

ISBN 0-449-15011-9

Manufactured in the United States of America

First Edition: June 2000

10   9   8   7   6   5   4   3   2   1

This one's for
Bill and Marbeth Foster

To Begin With . . .

Someone was dead. Lady Margaret Priam knew that right away. The people staring down over the edge of the terrace to the street and gabbling incoherently to one another must have known it, too. They could all see the crumpled shape on the street, not quite wedged between two black cars that reflected the lights under the maroon canopy into the apartment building. The lights were too dim, however, to identify anything about the body on the ground.

A silver Mylar balloon had detached itself from its mooring and was floating above the terrace, against the dark night sky where only a few stars managed to defeat the glow of Manhattan. She heard a tinkling splatter of broken glass. Someone had dropped a goblet. Then a cascade of metal and china. A waiter had dropped a serving tray. These were minor distractions that didn't penetrate the consciousness of the crowd leaning over the terrace parapet.

It was sixteen or seventeen stories from the terrace to the street, and now she heard the faint sirens wafting up from below. Someone—probably De Vere, who had been a guest tonight—had had the presence of mind to telephone. Certainly the guests hadn't thought to tear themselves away from the sensation. At least help was coming, but surely there was no help to be given, not now.

Margaret looked around her. These were all familiar faces, but pale and twisted by fear and concern. Their party clothes seemed to have wilted in just the few moments since the fall. Not all of the faces she expected to see were there, however. She looked for a slinky gold dress, a dark head of hair. A regal slash of crimson. Those she was seeking simply weren't there.

Prince Paul Castrocani left the crowd and came to Margaret's side.

"How could this happen?" he said. "Everyone was just standing there at the edge of the terrace, waiting for the cake, and then . . . My mother isn't going to care for this at all."

Then she saw his mother, Carolyn Sue Castrocani Hoopes, an airy vision in the palest pink, her blond hair a massive pile of genuinely Big Texas hair. An unseemly show of jewels sparkled in the multicolored fairy lights that decorated the terrace.

"He didn't even get to cut the birthday cake," she said with disapproval. The multitiered cake had just moments before been rolled onto the terrace on a wheeled tea wagon. Many of the candles still burned, but a few had sputtered out in the cool September breeze that stirred the air high above Park Avenue, and Manhattan spread out around them. The windows of the facing buildings showed lighted panes, and a few curious onlookers peeping out from behind drawn curtains.

"Surely that's not the most important matter at this moment," Margaret said. She noticed Dr. Dale Reeves, dentist to stars of many firmaments, looking wistfully at his birthday cake, but only for a moment. Then he marched to his guests with a grim face and spoke up.

"Let's everybody move away from the edge," he said. "The authorities are coming up now, and they don't want anything disturbed." With the help of Sam De Vere of the New York City Police, Margaret's escort and an unwilling guest at this event, Dr. Reeves started to herd the guests into the huge living room of his monstrously large apartment. They moved reluctantly, and Margaret imagined that they were a class of recalcitrant children who didn't want to leave a particularly bloody fistfight on the playground. She could hear people asking pointless questions: Who had fallen? How could it have happened?

"I never liked the girl. Was it her?"

"Is it Roberta? She was so depressed after Dale spoke."

"Was she pushed? Who wanted her dead?"

"I think she jumped."

"I knew there was something wrong about this whole business. Roberta told me only yesterday . . ."

"Where's Lucy? Is it her down there?"

"Has anyone seen Susan? She and her mother were at odds lately. . . ."

"I don't want to get mixed up in anything to do with the police."

"Roberta's parties are always disasters, but this is too much."

The party guests moved inside, where Margaret could see De Vere conferring with uniformed and plainclothes officers. It didn't seem to matter that these people were all from the best social circles of New York. They all behaved like rubberneckers at a multiple-auto accident.

And they were just like everybody else: enamored of the thrill of a hideous tragedy.

Carolyn Sue said to Margaret, "I didn't see a thing, did you? I was talking to someone, and just heard a scream. I never should have sent Lucia Rose up here among these barbarians. Poor little thing. Where has she got to?" She looked around, then at Margaret, stricken. "Lord, that's not her down there, is it?"

"We don't know. Let's let De Vere sort it out. He'll tell us whatever he can," she said sensibly.

Lady Margaret Priam was almost always sensible, although just now she felt that a cloak of unease mixed with a sense of danger had enveloped her. She didn't know who had been killed, or why.

All she knew for certain was that somebody was dead.

Chapter 1

Not very long before, Lady Margaret had been warned, not precisely about this event, but still, it had been a warning of sorts.

"She's after you. Be afraid, be very afraid."

"Paul, is that you?" Lady Margaret Priam had absolutely no doubt that it was Prince Paul Castrocani on the other end of the line. "Who is after me?"

There was silence, and then a sigh, a deep, dramatic Italianate sigh, and Paul said, "My mother."

"Ah," Margaret said, "and why would Carolyn Sue be 'after' me?"

"She wants a favor."

"Then of course she shall have it. She's done more than her fair share of favors for me." Then she added quickly, "Nothing to do with real estate, I hope." Carolyn Sue's decision to become a real estate mogul had once embroiled Margaret in a messy situation.

"I think not. She has chosen to allow Mr. Trump to take all the glory, and for her present holdings, she has hired a whole pack of professionals to supervise the giant earthmovers and evict the poor old grandmothers who fail to pay their rent. It's more of a social favor she wants, I believe."

5

"Is that all? Society runs on favors asked and received. Should I ring her? Is she here in New York or in Texas?"

"She's presently in San Francisco, not at home. She will telephone you. I merely wanted to warn you."

"But why should I be afraid? She's done so much for me."

"That is the point, and you know my mother. Even if you don't care to do the favor, she'll wear you down until you agree. It is rather how the Mafia operates back in Italy, and once the Mafia cleverly disguised as Carolyn Sue does a favor for you, you are obliged to return it on demand."

"I can handle Carolyn Sue," Margaret said, although she frowned to herself and wondered if she really could. She didn't quite believe that the blond and beautiful Carolyn Sue Hoopes, formerly the wife of Prince Aldo Castrocani, operated like the Mafia, but she was very, very rich and from the cradle had been accustomed to having her way in spite of parents; nursemaids; well-intentioned friends and their mothers; husbands; her son, Paul; as well as the lowliest of shopgirls, the loftiest bankers and investment counselers; and the pastor of her family-endowed Baptist church. Indeed, she almost fancied herself as a match for God on high.

In a friendship existing only a few years, she had as yet only modestly tested the will of the British aristocracy in the form of Lady Margaret Priam. Margaret straightened her shoulders. The Empire hadn't been built on caving in to the demands of colonials like Carolyn Sue. Margaret, with the blood of the Empire coursing through her veins, wouldn't let the side down. "You have no idea exactly what this favor would be?"

"Something to do with a job, I think," Paul said vaguely,

and Margaret sensed that he was torn between telling her exactly what he knew and letting her twist in the wind until Carolyn Sue Castrocani Hoopes arranged her busy schedule and telephoned to ask her favor in her own way.

"A job for precisely whom? Me? You? Carolyn Sue?" The last was, of course, unthinkable. Carolyn Sue had never worked a second in her life, unless one considered her long-ago marriage to Paul's father, Prince Aldo, a true job.

On the other hand, Paul was always being placed by his mother in an unsuitable job in a difficult profession where he lasted for mere nanoseconds, and he and Margaret were at leisure just now. Both could use gainful employment.

"Someone else," Paul said. "I really do not know the details." And that was that, although Margaret was convinced he knew more than he was telling.

Paul was a close enough contemporary for her to use her seniority as an excuse to make him tell. But for now she surrendered to his refusal, and instead made firm arrangements to dine with him later in the week. She genuinely liked young Prince Paul, and enjoyed his company, and they had certainly shared some gruesome moments. Still, she was careful not to mention Sam De Vere, who shared Paul's rent-free apartment, conveniently owned by Carolyn Sue, when he wasn't enforcing Quality of Life issues in Manhattan as a member of the police force. If De Vere had chosen to disappear for a time or just retreat into silence as far as she was concerned, she wasn't about to indicate to Paul that she'd noticed and been hurt by his absence. She suspected that men gossiped as much as women, so she didn't care to have Paul and De Vere discussing her feelings.

Still, Margaret was relieved that Carolyn Sue wasn't going to offer her a job, not that she was terribly occupied at present. She looked around her comfortable apartment, and sighed. It was expensive to keep this place on Manhattan's Upper East Side. Lady Margaret Priam admitted to herself that she, like Prince Aldo Castrocani in his Renaissance villa outside of Rome, was a comparatively impoverished aristocrat, getting by on a modest inheritance, an expatriate Brit who'd been settled in New York City for nearly a decade, dining out on her title and upper-class English accent, her undeniably good manners, and maybe her blond good looks. She was willing to join committees and work hard for worthy causes. People liked her, but being a gem on society's tiara didn't pay the bills.

Except for informal fees she'd earned for helping others resolve difficult problems, she hadn't had a real job for several years, not since she worked at Bedros Kasparian's antiques shop.

No, she certainly wouldn't care to be under the supervision of Paul's mother, who was a dedicated controller of others' lives, but that might simply be the result of an existence supported by extreme wealth, where wishes and whims were instantly gratified, and no delays were brooked. Margaret understood that. The aristocratic milieu she'd grown up in hadn't had the kind of money that Carolyn Sue was born to, but they were every bit as strong-willed and demanding. Nevertheless the two women were good friends, even aside from Margaret's friendship with Paul. Margaret knew that Carolyn Sue was the one person she could always count on for support, no matter how unlikely the request. If Carolyn Sue needed a favor, it would be petty of Margaret to refuse.

Margaret picked up a volume on art history and found her place. She was taking a few courses so as to be prepared to work again in the art and antiques business, should Bedros decide to reopen. She had liked going to the shop, meeting customers, persuading them to purchase expensive Oriental knicknacks most of them didn't need. The serious collectors, of course, relied on Bedros, who knew everything, whereas Margaret knew mostly what looked good.

Suddenly, she shut the book firmly and admitted that she was bored. Her finances really were in terrible shape, so if Carolyn Sue should offer her a job, she'd have to take it.

It was a rainy fall day, with a heavy gray cloud cover that obscured the tops of the tall buildings surrounding her apartment house. Not a day to wander the streets, and window-shop along Madison Avenue.

She wondered if any of her friends were similarly bored and at loose ends. Who to call for a diversion? Who might be free to lunch? Should she see if there was a possibility of an appointment with her manicurist? Her best friend, Dianne Stark, was in Los Angeles, so there was no hope of companionship there. Since her off-again, on-again romance with Sam De Vere appeared to be definitely off, there wasn't even a hope that she could see him that evening. Most of her other so-called friends were too occupied with their own affairs—domestic, romantic, charitable—to fit in a spur-of-the-moment adventure.

Margaret continued to sit on her chintz-covered sofa

with the heavy book on her lap, trying to think of something to do with herself. She should have kept Paul on the line until she'd thought of something entertaining they could do together. A museum? No, Paul had grown up in a house near Rome that boasted a reputed Raphael on the wall, and he'd played in the bustling streets of a city that was close to being a museum of all Renaissance art and classical civilization. He now avoided museums religiously.

A film? No, movies in the daytime disoriented her, and she didn't care to search the clothing racks at Bergdorf's or to check out the boutiques on Madison Avenue alone.

Stop it, she said to herself. It was not very long ago that I was sitting in Carolyn Sue's unspeakably white drawing room in that huge house of hers in Dallas, thinking that I was living a pointless life here in New York, joining committees, choosing menus and flowers for charity events, listening to all the silly gossip, lunching, and pampering myself. I was determined to change, and look what I'm back to. I'm feeling sorry for myself and I haven't been doing a thing to change anything.

She closed her eyes, and only briefly considered the grave immorality of napping before noon.

Ring! It was two when the phone rang and woke her. Not surprisingly, it was Carolyn Sue.

"Darlin', I sure do miss y'all in New York." Margaret had never been convinced that Carolyn Sue's accent was genuine. Possibly it had been developed years before to mask her somewhat inadequate Italian.

"Where are you?" Margaret struggled to shake off the lassitude that engulfed her.

"I'm sitting here in San Francisco, thinkin' about gettin' out of the city and maybe takin' a spin up through the wine country. How's that boy of mine doin'? Still fixin' to marry that rich English tart?"

Margaret didn't know what to say. The Honourable Georgina Farfaine was certainly English, rather well-off and perhaps a bit on the wild side, but "tart" seemed excessive. Margaret knew from Carolyn Sue's own Estee Lauder–tinted lips that she had been quite taken with Georgina when Paul had brought her home to meet the family. And after all, hadn't the youthful Carolyn Sue chosen a titled family when she decided to wed? Lord Farfaine, Georgina's father, was surely as distinguished as any princely Castrocani. Georgina would be a good match for Paul, if it ever came to pass. Love had blossomed perhaps, but commitment was still a mere immature grape on the vine.

Margaret mentioned none of those things, but merely said, "He hasn't said anything lately, but he did ring me just this morning to say you needed a favor."

"A bitty one," Carolyn Sue said. "You're just the person to help me out. It has to do with one o' my pals in Dallas, my most precious friend really, we were debs together, and went to the University of Texas together. . . ."

Margaret blinked. It had never occurred to her that Carolyn Sue had made a stab at higher education.

"We were both Kappa Alpha Theta, too, and that's real sisterhood. She was just the most precious thing in the world. Things were so simple and fun back then, you know, before we had responsibilities for husbands and children, keeping a lovely home, working for the Junior League. . . ."

Apparently it was going to take a while for Carolyn Sue to get to the point, so Margaret conjured up an image of Carolyn Sue as a pretty blond University of

Texas coed decked out in all the finery her rich father could afford, cheering on the football team without perhaps understanding anything that was occurring on the field. Maybe the game part wasn't all that important. Well, that was all right, since Margaret herself had achieved very little understanding of American football, being unable to grasp the desire of masses of people to sit in a stadium during a snowstorm while king-sized men with firm round bottoms ran to and fro in pursuit of a brown ovoid ball. Carolyn Sue must have enjoyed the dressing up and the camaraderie of game day, and the handsome youth who escorted her.

"The reason I called you, Margaret, is this."

Margaret allowed the packed, cheering stadium to fade and attended to Carolyn Sue.

"My friend had a daughter, just as darlin' as her momma."

"Had?"

"The girl still is, but poor Gracie died when she was thrown by a horse out at the ranch when Lucy Rose was just a teenager. Now she's ready to take her proper place in society in Dallas. But that's the problem. I don't understand it myself, but the girl is eager as can be to move up there with all those Yankees. She wants to live in New York City." Carolyn Sue sounded truly puzzled. "She has a perfectly lovely life in Dallas. Her daddy's pretty well fixed, and there's parties and boys all over the place, and I don't know what all."

Yes, Margaret thought, "what all" like the flagship store of Neiman Marcus right there in her backyard. "I suppose," Margaret said cautiously, "young people today want to get a taste of everything, and the place that has everything is New York. You spend enough time here yourself to know that."

"I'm not a kid, like Lucy," Carolyn Sue said. "And it's different for me. I need to be there for social reasons, to see my friends and to look out for my business interests and such. I'm too old to be infected by liberal ideas and the kind of craziness that goes on up there. Lucy Rose is young and impressionable, a real innocent. 'Course, she insisted on leavin' the University at home and goin' up north to college. It was someplace in Massachusetts." Carolyn Sue made it sound as though Lucy Rose had chosen the University of Moscow, with a major in Marxism. "Still, she's pretty as a cream puff, and about as tough. I'm pretty sure all those liberal Boston ideas didn't get under her skin." Carolyn Sue hesitated. "Not too much, anyhow. But Boston at least has some real fine people. New York is different. It's dangerous. She needs to be protected."

"And you'd like to have me chaperone her when she comes here."

"Why, I never thought of it that way, Margaret honey. I guess I was hopin' you'd keep half an eye on her, but what I was wantin' you to do was to help her find a job."

Margaret didn't trample on Carolyn Sue's hopes by reminding her that she couldn't even find herself a job, let alone a job for a deb from Texas, who had . . . what kind of skills could little Lucy have to get herself into the competitive New York job market?

"What can she do?" Margaret asked.

"Do?" Carolyn Sue sounded puzzled. "Oh, you mean what can she do so that someone will hire her?"

"Exactly."

"Well, she did graduate from that Massachusetts college, but I don't know what she studied there. Nothin' of any use, I imagine."

"Has she ever had a job?"

"Why, sure she has. After her momma died, I kinda looked out for her, teachin' her things she needed to know, 'cause her daddy, Big Ed, was a pretty busy man. Very active in politics at the time. Little Lucy stepped right in and took over the household. She was her daddy's hostess all the years after Grace died. And Big Ed Grant's a mighty important person in these parts, so there was lots of entertainin' and business meetings and people coming to stay. His place is a real big spread, but Lucy managed it all like a real trooper. The ladies were so impressed, and the gentlemen all took to her. I guess you could say Lucy's a born organizer and an expeditor of the first order. Nowadays, Big Ed's cuttin' back some on his socializing, and there's even talk about him remarrying. Edna Anne Wright. You wouldn't know her, but she's got her hooks into him somethin' fierce. Anyhow, Lucy Rose will have nothin' to do if there's another woman in the house. Edna has her own way of doin' things. So now Lucy says she's bored with Dallas." Carolyn Sue seemed to find that incomprehensible. "I was thinkin', Margaret, that one of those committee ladies you know up there in New York might need an assistant, a pretty little girl to keep things in order, call the right people at the right time, order the stationery from Tiffany's, keep track of engagements, check the accounts to be sure the housekeeper and the cook don't steal too much. . . ."

"A social secretary, in other words?"

"That's about it," Carolyn Sue said. "I'd like to see

Lucy fall in love with the social ramble. Right now she doesn't like to follow the rules sometimes, and she needs to be taught what the rules are in a place like New York. She's smart, and she likes to be the leader of whatever set she's runnin' around with. I was thinkin' she ought to be helpin' out somebody who's top drawer in the social scene up there since she's determined to go. She needs to learn the ropes from the best. Then maybe she'll meet a boy from a real nice family to marry. I don't know that Big Ed would cotton to a Yankee boy, but we'll worry about crossing that bridge when we get to it. Besides, I can handle Big Ed. He was kinda sweet on me when we were in college, 'fore he met Lucy's momma. If Lucy should marry one of those nose-stuck-in-the-air, old-money Yankee types, she's gotta be ready to take her rightful place in society. Good hard trainin' is what it takes. Think you can do somethin' for her?"

"I might," Margaret said hesitantly as she searched her mental list of acquaintances in need of Lucy's organizational skills, for someone who was looking for a social secretary. "But you know just about everyone here that I do."

"Sure, I know them, but I don't keep up with who's doin' what and who needs somebody like Lucy Rose. You understand."

"Why don't you give me a number where I can call you if I think of someone, and we can go from there?"

"Here's my mobile number. The thing goes wherever I go, although I do shut it off when I'm eating out or at the opera. They get kinda cranky here in San Fran if a phone rings while the soprano's doin' her dyin' act."

"I just thought . . ." Margaret stopped. She had thought

of a possible future employer for the darlin' Lucy, but decided to hold back for the moment.

"Thought what?"

"Where's the girl going to live? I mean, I'd love to have her here with me, but I don't have a lot of room, and she's probably used to having her own space." And lots of it, she added to herself.

"Maybe the lady who takes her on will have a little maid's room for Lucy. But her daddy can afford to rent her a place, no problem there. There might even be space in one of my buildings." Carolyn Sue had invested in several Manhattan apartment buildings, among other business interests in the city. "Well, I'm glad everything's settled. I'm going back to Dallas in a couple of days, so you call me at home and tell me what the arrangements are. Or I'll call you, I'm that anxious to get her settled. To tell you the truth, Margaret honey, I don't like what I've been hearin' about her companions. Big Ed is frantic with worry that she's taken up with the wrong sort. We'll get little Lucy packed off to New York, and she'll make new friends. You take care now, you hear?"

Margaret hung up, thinking that friendship with the likes of Carolyn Sue carried a lot of baggage.

Arrangements? None to speak of. She'd spend a couple of days to find an employer for a cream puff who was an expeditor without references except from her father, Big Ed, and Carolyn Sue Castrocani Hoopes. The latter, at least, had clout in New York social circles, and Margaret had her title. That was good for something. Little Lucy would wing into La Guardia with a ton of Vuitton luggage, to spend a few nights here with Margaret while they scanned the real estate pages of *The New York Times* and pounded the avenues and cross streets looking at apartments.

Paul could help by introducing her to suitable friends. If little Lucy was so dear to Carolyn Sue, Paul and she must be old friends. And he must have known all about his mother's plan to have Margaret find her a job.

Arrangements would be made.

Chapter 2

In fact, one or two names had come to Margaret while she was talking to Carolyn Sue. Three names, actually. Margaret herself had worked for a short time as an assistant to a top interior designer, but had withdrawn in the face of hordes of perpetually dissatisfied women clients and disdainful purveyors of luxury furnishings. Giovanni Millennia had begged her to stay on, but the pay she received for suffering abuse from his clients' total insecurity about the color of their walls and the choice of window treatments had made the venture generally unpleasant.

"I have my own work to do," she'd lied the day she resigned. Giovanni had sighed mightily and released her. Surely he still needed the sort of assistant she'd been, and she hadn't heard that he had taken anyone on. Maybe little Lucy was just the ticket. Giovanni was certainly no threat to the child's morals, unless the impact of divinely sensitive and aesthetically correct decorators and their hangers-on could do her damage. There were other interior designers she knew. Bobby Henley was a love, but she'd never consider thrusting Lucy into the orbit of the terrifying Eloise Corbell, who had readily turned her hand to decorating after her stint as Madame Ambassador had ended with the infamous lingonberry affair. Still, Eloise had the kind of status that would please Carolyn Sue. The Mistress of Mauve, Juana de los Angeles, was a bit déclassé, and Godfrey Helms was, in a word, impossible. She'd ask Giovanni.

In the end, Margaret decided that hauling Lalique objets to be inspected for possible incorporation into the design scheme of a drawing room wasn't quite what Carolyn Sue had in mind for her young protégé, precious though she might be, although Giovanni would treat her well.

Margaret thought about socially connected ladies who might suit little Lucy. Rather than Giovanni, it was someone like Candy Pierce or Roberta Reeves who would suit the bill. Candy was a possibility, but she was still making her way to the top of the social heap. Roberta was definitely a person who needed to have things handled for her. Goodness knew she had social position to burn, sat on the board of trustees of almost every important city institution, and her good works were endlessly reported, not the least because her husband, Dr. Dale Reeves, a strikingly handsome dentist, of all things, had wide prominence of his own, ministering to the dental ills of really important (and rich) people.

The key to unlocking little Lucy's job opportunity, as Margaret saw it, was the fact that Roberta's committees, of which there were many, were widely rumored to be the epitome of disorganization. Roberta was well known for exhibiting a breathtakingly done-in-the-knick-of-time approach when pulling off major charity events. Very unnerving for all concerned when someone forgot to order the vegetarian meal requested by the charity's biggest contributor or when the flowers arrived a day early and wilted before the party got under way.

There was a downside to the choice of Roberta. The gossip mill regularly ground out tales of Reeves family dustups. The Reeves' grown daughter, Susan, and their adult son, Gregory, had once made tabloid headlines with a messy public confrontation over some trivial matter. Margaret had heard that a gun was involved and that the siblings no longer spoke to each other.

Margaret had also heard, but didn't pay much heed to, the tales of Dale Reeves' womanizing. He had a mistress, the editor of a glossy fashion magazine. Such a manly reputation is often desirable, and is nurtured for its own peculiar social value. One assumed that a noted dentist probably needed a bit of glamour to enhance his position, and offset the generally negative feelings people had about dentists, who are not glamorous per se. At least Dr. Dale hadn't stirred up any scandals by having publicized affairs with his patients. Margaret thought that dentistry-inspired romance was unlikely, because the man in question frequently had his hands in one's mouth. At least it wasn't the sort of profession that called the good doctor out of bed at all hours to attend to life-threatening emergencies.

Dale Reeves did have patients who were celebrities, including film stars and musicians, and even the stray titled European, so he clearly knew all the best people, and Roberta would certainly know them as well. That was probably why she was in demand as an organizer of events to benefit worthy causes. She could lean on bold-face names to attend her fêtes, and lure in ticket buyers. Who wouldn't want to rub shoulders with Sharon Stone or Brad Pitt, Jack Nicholson or Michael Jordan over cocktails?

Margaret herself had visited Dr. Dale once professionally, but had found his substantial fees off-putting. But he was charming in a social setting, while Roberta was hard as a rock. She supposed that as Roberta was pushing middle age, and middle age was pushing back, she felt herself at risk in the trophy wife ringtoss. Maybe that was why she apparently accepted her husband's mistress. Lorna herself was a mature woman, and not a fresh-faced young vixen with visions of snaring a well-off man, albeit a dentist.

For a moment, Margaret wondered if she dare toss a naïve child from Texas into this mix, but concluded that if little Lucy could handle a houseful of her father's friends and political figures, and remain as precious as ever, she shouldn't worry. Of course, there was still the matter of persuading Roberta to hire this paragon. Carolyn Sue was inclined to exaggerate when it was a means of getting her way.

In fact, Margaret knew nothing of little Lucy, except that her momma had been a pal of Carolyn Sue's, and precious thing that she was, she was highly thought of as a substitute hostess for her daddy. What did Big Ed himself do, anyhow? Was there a Little Ed?

Margaret grabbed the phone and dialed Paul. Fortunately, he also had not found anything to do outside his apartment in Chelsea in the building owned by his mother. When he answered, she was busily wondering again if Carolyn Sue had another Manhattan apartment building where little Lucy could find shelter.

"*Pronto,*" Paul said lazily.

"It's Margaret," she said. "And do you imagine you're

ensconced in *Roma,* with your *pronto*s to answer the phone?"

"At least you didn't have to speak to one of those awful answering machines. I am homesick," Paul said. "Georgina and I are thinking of going to Italy to visit my father again. He likes her, and I like Rome in September. The weather is still fine and many of the tourists have returned home to Japan. The problem is that 2000 is a Holy Year, so there will be more tourists than ever, no matter what the month."

"The tourists will all be at the Vatican, visiting the Pope."

"They will be everywhere, crowding the Spanish Steps, eating in my favorite restaurants, gaping at the Forum. We shall have to hide ourselves away at the villa."

"I understand your concern, but listen. Carolyn Sue called and asked her favor, but there was no need for me to be afraid. She merely wants me to find a job for the daughter of some old friend of hers who died when the girl was a teenager."

"Little Lucy Rose Grant, that would be."

"You do know her. I thought you would. I need to know more about her."

"I warned you to be afraid. There is nothing else to add."

"Afraid of little Lucy? She sounds an ordinary sort of girl, who just wants to bask in the bright lights of New York."

"You know I am not a good judge of women, Margaret, except for you and Georgina. I've known Lucia much of my life, or as much of it as I've spent in Texas, and she's not at all ordinary, at least not by Dallas standards."

"Go on. I need to know everything."

Paul seemed to hesitate. "I can only go by what my mother has indicated, even if I cannot understand the significance of all of it." Margaret waited to hear the worst.

"Lucia Rose has been known to wear white after Labor Day, and according to my mother, this is simply not done."

"But I've seen Carolyn Sue decked out in white from her head to her toes, at all times of the year."

"In the privacy of her home perhaps," Paul said, "which in any case is mostly white itself."

Indeed it is, Margaret thought, even to the baby grand piano. "Still, that doesn't sound so dangerous, or something to be afraid of."

"There is more. I was told with great disapproval that she refused to be the queen of some social event. Happily, I am ten years older and was away from Texas during Lucy's formative social years, so I was not required to escort her to anything," Paul said. "My mother did not make too much of her refusal, since she herself was already a genuine princess, but such a step on the part of someone like Lucy is considered very bad behavior among Texas ladies of good family. Being the queen of a festivity, or even a mere princess of her court, is a high honor, not easily dismissed."

"I am still not convinced that this signifies a girl to fear," Margaret said. "I certainly would have refused to be Queen at home in England, had the opportunity been offered, and you know what becomes of princesses there. It's not worth the trouble."

"I think," Paul said darkly, "that being honored as temporary royalty is far more important in Dallas than in England. In any case, Lucia has an enduring bad reputation. For one thing, she left the University of Texas to study in Boston. The idea that a Texas maiden would venture to such a place only added to my mother's concern about her. If Lucy's mother had been alive, such a thing would never have happened. Carolyn Sue felt responsible. I don't believe she comported herself well in Boston, even according to the lax standards of the Yankees, but I don't know the details. And there were other things, once she came back to Dallas."

"Other things?"

"By then, my mother and father were divorced, and Carolyn Sue had married Benton Hoopes, who effectively cut me off from the really substantial allowance my mother provided, so I myself was forced to live in Texas."

Margaret remembered Paul's tales of European jet-set life when his funds were plentiful, and then his sadness when they were terminated by his stepfather.

"So I was thrown together with Lucy as circumstances required. Now and then I actually was expected to escort her to various events, but dearly as my mother wished us to become an item, or indeed to marry, it was not to be. Lucy's taste in men did not include the likes of me, and her interests ran to . . . well, a different sort of man. It was considered doubtful behavior. My mother always felt it was because she chose not to be blond."

Margaret scarcely grasped the importance of hair color since she was a natural blonde, so she concentrated on the mention of doubtful behavior.

"What sort of behavior?"

"Everyone blamed it on her northern education. She seemed to prefer the company of Latinos, you know,

Mexicans, of which there are quite a number in Texas. Now, I have Latin blood by virtue of my father, but for some reason, Lucy and I did not hit it off."

"And these Latinos led her to 'doubtful behavior,' or were they it?"

"Not exactly," Paul said. "She was interested in a boy called Filipe Garcia, who had three beautiful and terrifying sisters. The Garcia sisters were dedicated to arousing their people to better their lives. I think one of the Garcia sisters had attended the same Massachusetts college that Lucy eventually chose. In any event, Filipe and his sisters got her interested in matters concerning the Latino culture and the people. Lucy was always daring, drawn to danger, willing to take risks. I suppose she must have a social conscience as well. Anyhow, she helped organize labor unions; she led protests about living conditions. She gave inflammatory interviews to the media.

"Big Ed didn't care for this, since he was involved in state and city politics and hated the publicity. Fortunately, she was never arrested at her demonstrations, or if she was, Big Ed pulled strings to get her off. Then there were rumors that she had been involved in some criminal activity, probably driving the getaway car. Filipe was arrested for something, but if she was involved, somehow her father managed to extricate her from that difficulty as well. My mother would know all the details, and she could fill you in on the time Lucy was involved with that young politician. It all came out when his wife raised a stink. It's the kind of gossip Carolyn Sue loves. She can justify flaring her nostrils in outrage at what today's youth has come to.

"Honestly, Margaret, I didn't know Lucy well then,

and I certainly know nothing of her now. My mother says she's ambitious, but for what I do not know. She has plenty of money, although not as much as my mother. She could try to take her place in society in Dallas, but she may have stepped beyond acceptability. I suppose she wants to come to New York to be free from all the censorious looks and the rules that women of my mother's set have established and she likes to break. In spite of what I've said, she's probably perfectly nice, well behaved in company, and she's certainly attractive. . . ."

"Although not blond," Margaret said. "Well, I'll see what I can do for her, unless you think she's likely to steal from her employer."

Paul laughed. "I think you are safe there. I don't believe that Lucia Rose is interested in stealing material goods. There's enough else to steal in New York. I warned you to be afraid."

Chapter 3

*M*argaret had the feeling that Carolyn Sue expected fast action on little Lucy's situation, so rather than puttering around trying to think of something to do, she decided to examine her tiny guest bedroom and determine whether it was in shape to receive a wealthy young lady from Texas.

Alas, it was more like a closet, with no window and only a single bed, an unpleasant lamp, a small bureau with a mirror, and some hooks on the wall for hanging garments. But the walls were painted a cheerful yellow, a nice print of a summer garden was hung over the bed, and a bright area rug covered the polished wood floor. It was pleasant if small, but it had never housed more than an overnight guest who lived out of a suitcase.

It will have to do, she thought. I'm not giving up my big, comfortable bed. And after all, it's only for a day or two.

The white bedspread was clean and unwrinkled, and the puffy yellow-and-blue pillows gave the occupant a place to sit back in comfort. Too bad there wasn't room for a chair. She'd buy some flowers to further brighten the room.

Margaret was not entirely comforted by Paul's description of little Lucy, but felt that Carolyn Sue would not be much more forthcoming about the girl. She had to take it on trust that Lucy would perform as advertised, and decided to ring Roberta Reeves in the morning.

New York ladies were seldom at home in the afternoons since they had to attend to so much time-consuming self-maintenance, and Roberta, who hovered around the middle of middle age, was likely to need a lot of maintenance. Hair, skin, feet, clothes, fingers, and toes required attention on a regular basis. Early evenings were usually taken up with preparations for going out to fashionable gatherings later in the evening—dinners, the theatre, cocktail parties, clandestine rendezvous, or gala festivities—again a question of organizing hair, skin, feet, clothes, fingers, and toes so as to appear in peak condition, ready to be photographed for *Vanity Fair, W, Town & Country,* and other glossy publications that featured photos of the wealthy and famous at play. Tomorrow morning, unless Roberta was recovering from her evening out on the town, Margaret could surely reach her before noon and Going-Out-to-Lunch-with-the-Ladies-Who-Lunch time.

Just to be on the safe side in terms of an occupation for Lucy, Margaret decided to go around to see Giovanni at his interior design offices, in case he had a fetch-the-sample-book sort of job that Lucy might fill. Even if he didn't and Roberta failed her, Giovanni might be persuaded to give Lucy some busy work until something more suitable came along. Surely once word got about that Margaret had a gofer to let, someone would scoop up little Lucy, unsightly brunette hair and all.

Margaret strolled down Third Avenue in the late afternoon under chilly September skies. The weather forecast promised better days to come. She reached the cluster of buildings that housed several interior design firms and many shops that were open only to the decorating trade and that purveyed fabrics, furniture, crystal chandeliers, and antique furnishings. Giovanni had the second floor of a rather ramshackle corner building that housed a noisy pizza shop at street level.

"Margaret, what a surprise! How good to see you." Giovanni kissed Margaret on both cheeks and sat her down in a fanciful armchair upholstered in magenta, summoned an assistant to bring chilled flutes of ProSecco and a little tray of pastries, and sat down in his own armchair, this one a bright lemon yellow. Giovanni had for a time decorated exclusively in shades of gray, but he seemed to have turned to bright colors for inspiration.

"How I miss you and your exquisite taste," he said mournfully with just a touch of an accent. Giovanni was not, of course, authentically Italian, rather pure American, the former John Miller, a product of Brooklyn. He played his assumed role well, however, and his clients were as delighted with his work as any clients of interior designers ever were.

He waved away the lithe youth who had brought the refreshments. "Enough, my pet," he said, and the youth, a remarkably handsome specimen, pouted and withdrew. "He's a new friend who wants to learn the business," Giovanni said. "Possible talent for design, but we'll see. What can I do for you, Margaret? Have you reconsidered returning to me?"

"I'm not cut out for the decorating business," Margaret said. "But I was wondering if you needed someone to assist you. Someone who might do the sort of thing I used to do. There's a lovely young woman . . ."

Giovanni shrugged. "There are always boring tasks that need to be done, but business is slow just now, and I can't take on anyone new. Not even the loveliest young woman on the continent. Besides, Alberto suits me." His eyes flickered toward the door through which the youth had departed, and Margaret decided that Alberto— or probably just plain Al—suited Giovanni in all possible ways.

"Carolyn Sue asked me to find some little job for the daughter of a friend of hers, who's moving to New York," Margaret said. She explained about poor little Lucy and her desire to get out of Dallas. "She wouldn't ask for much money. I understand her father is quite well-off."

"And I understand the desire to leave Dallas, naturally," he said. "I have been there often enough to feel that it leaves much to be desired. If your young woman is truly lovely and rich, I can easily imagine her cutting a swath through the younger social set. Surely she doesn't need a job at all, whereas Alberto does, being both poor and lovely."

"She has to do something," Margaret said. "If I'm going to be partly responsible for her, I can't have her lying in bed all day eating chocolates." Then she explained her alternate plan to have little Lucy work for someone like Roberta Reeves at a nominal salary, handling various chores and keeping Roberta's busy schedule in order.

"I wonder if it's wise to put an innocent young woman into that household," Giovanni said thoughtfully. "I did a room or two for Roberta a few years back, and caught a whiff of simmering tensions in the household. The good dentist is a smooth one. He even fixed a little problem I had with a tooth, at a remarkably high cost." He tapped a gleaming, possibly capped, front tooth. "All the same, I would not trust my daughter in his company, should the unlikely case occur that I had a daughter. Darling Margaret, don't look so downcast. I don't believe his tastes run to nubile youngsters. He has a very distinguished lady friend that Roberta appears to tolerate quite well. It has been going on for years and years. And everybody knows about Roberta."

Margaret blinked. "I don't." But she had heard something. Ah, yes, a brief but torrid romance with Richard Centner, the one-time partner of Peter Anton, the man who made a name for himself by rehabilitating old town houses about Manhattan. "I do remember hearing something," she said, "but surely that was long ago."

"I shall not gossip," Giovanni said. "Discretion is all-important in my business. Ask Poppy Dill if you need to know the current status."

"I don't, really. I just want to place the girl somewhere. I don't want her in my hair for the next few months."

"Then call Roberta and put it to her straight. Either she takes the girl or risks the wrath of Carolyn Sue Hoopes. That should solve the problem nicely. Alberto! More ProSecco!" At the sound of his raised voice, Alberto appeared instantly with a bottle in his hand.

"No more for me," Margaret said. "Too much champagnelike substance in the afternoon makes me drowsy." But Giovanni held out his glass, and gazed fondly at Alberto as he topped off his drink. Margaret stood up. "I ought to get home to prepare my plea to Roberta."

"I wish I could accommodate the girl," Giovanni said,

"but it's simply impossible at this time. If you like, I can call a few people. Most of my fellow decorators are sufficiently tyrannical that their help doesn't stay long. Have you considered Bobby Henley?"

Margaret nodded. "And Madame Ambassador, and Juana, and Godfrey," she said.

"Not suitable at all," Giovanni said, "and rather bad decorators, at that. But don't fret. There are often openings."

"Let me try Roberta first, but do let me know if you think of anybody else."

"Of course, I will put my mind to work. It can't hurt to have the goodwill of Carolyn Sue. I understand she has a very large house in Texas that is often in need of redecorating. I would enjoy the challenge after all these jobs for Long Island social climbers and Manhattan trophy wives who want to erase the memories of the lady who got there first. And remember, if you chose to return to me, I would not hesitate a moment to take you back. You were so good with those difficult women."

"I appreciate your confidence," Margaret said, "and I may return one day. I am going to need to go to work eventually to help support myself."

"Ah, but I understood you were to marry that . . . that good-looking police person and live in New Jersey."

Margaret sighed. "I don't think Sam is the marrying kind," she said. "And I'm not sure I am either. I've been alone for so long that I'm rather accustomed to that state."

"You can't live on charity benefits and idle cocktail conversation forever," Giovanni said sternly. At least he didn't say anything about her getting on in years, although his expression seemed to say that being in her mid-thirties and single was a fate worse than death.

"I have some things in mind," Margaret said. "I might go back to school full-time and learn a trade."

Giovanni threw back his head and laughed. "Lady Margaret Priam, the sister of the Earl of Brayfield, learns a trade. And what trade were you considering?"

"I'm good with animals," she said. "I might study veterinary medicine."

"Animals? You say you're good at riding difficult horses. Better to become a riding instructor, teaching spoiled adolescent girls to ride."

"It's a thought," Margaret said, and went on her way. Now that she was on Third Avenue near the Decorator's Building, she was also near Bloomingdale's, and it never hurt to give the place a glance or two.

As it happened, she found a sweet little lamp on the home furnishings floor that would do nicely for little Lucy's temporary abode. Then, in the linens department, she picked out some thick rosy pink towels that could be put to good use now and after Lucy departed, as she prayed she soon would.

She was close enough to her apartment to walk home, although her packages were bulky and should have been delivered. Still, there was no way of knowing either when Bloomingdale's would deliver or Lucy would be winging in.

She would be winging in soon, Margaret quickly discovered from the messages on her answering machine. One message was from Carolyn Sue, saying Lucy was eager to be in touch about her arrival, and another was from Lucy herself, giving her arrival time at La Guardia, and the American Airlines flight she would descend from.

And expressing the hope—more like a demand—that there would be a car awaiting her so she wouldn't have to bother with a nasty New York taxi.

Margaret played the message two or three times, to get a sense of the girl from her voice. No Texas accent, à la Carolyn Sue. In any case, Margaret imagined Carolyn Sue merely talked that way to give the impression of being a no-nonsense good ole gal from the dangerous frontier. Lucy sounded like a Mid-Atlantic debutante. Her message was entirely straightforward and business-like. And she didn't sound like Paul's image of a trouble-some lass.

It was easy enough to arrange for a car service to meet her flight, but things were moving fast. If she didn't find a job for Lucy, the girl would be hanging around the apartment all day. Well, the Madison Avenue designer boutiques were close by. Let her shop. She probably had a good résumé in that department, although the magic of Ralph Lauren, Nicole Miller, and Armani was likely to evaporate quickly.

Then there was the task of apartment hunting. And perhaps she should give a little party to introduce Lucy to the offspring of some of Margaret's friends to give her a start on a social career. Surely she could corral Paul into introducing Lucy to some of his friends. If the Honourable Georgina Farfaine happened to be in the city visiting Paul, she might be persuaded to take up sight-seeing duties for a day or two. No, that wasn't right. Georgina was English and not a native New Yorker. Margaret seemed to recall that she said she'd never even ridden on the subway during any of her frequent visits to New York. Georgina divided her time between England and the Caribbean island her family owned.

Margaret installed the lamp in the guest room and piled the new towels on a shelf in the tiny guest bathroom. She'd get the flowers tomorrow, after she'd convinced Roberta Reeves that the only thing lacking in her busy life was someone to sort out the problems and make it all run smoothly.

Chapter 4

It was amazingly easy to persuade Roberta to hire an unknown Texas girl, rich naturally, to become her Gal Monday-through-Friday. Possibly the mention of Carolyn Sue sealed the deal.

"I don't know that I have enough for her to do every single minute," Roberta said in that throaty voice of hers, "but I have sooo much to do right now. I'm chairing three really major committees, and it's all so disorganized. I don't know one event from the other. You say she's really good?"

"According to Carolyn Sue."

"There's no better judge of character. In my opinion. And if she's known the girl all her life . . . Now, I can't promise I can keep her on forever, and I really can't pay her much. Dale has been crabby about finances lately, although with the hours he works, we should be rolling in money. I'm always grateful that I need not worry about the financial demands of getting good dental care. So nice to have an expert in the family. Dale will have his hands full when Susan decides to have children. All those braces and things. Gregory's marriage is shaky right now, but Susan should be thinking of starting a family, even though I'm really too young to be a grandmother.

Still, I'd love some beautiful little kids around before I'm really too old."

"I don't believe Lucy needs much money, and she might have an occasional need to have a tooth looked after. It's more a question of keeping her busy. Eventually she may find something else she prefers to do, but it would be a real gesture of friendship if you could help me out."

"That part is easy, Margaret. You know I'd do anything to help friends like you, and Carolyn Sue. Where will she be living?" Roberta asked.

"She's staying with me at the start," Margaret said, "but I imagine she'll want to find her own place soon enough. I don't want to be her chaperone, or her roommate."

"You say she arrives the day after tomorrow? Bring her around the day after, and I'll see if she suits me. I mean, I can't just take her on sight unseen. What if she's monstrously ugly? That would never do."

Margaret could not imagine Carolyn Sue promoting a monstrously ugly person, but anything was possible. She hoped, though, that Roberta was able to tolerate non-blond females.

Little Lucy Rose's job interview was set for two in the afternoon, three days hence. Time enough later to check whether Roberta had a little maid's room that could harbor the girl.

Margaret hoped that Lucy would play her poker hand right and quickly, and become so indispensable that a room would be found for her in the Reeves household. Margaret knew that Roberta inhabited the obligatory (for a social figure) obscenely large apartment, and there was only her husband and herself to fill the space. The children were grown and gone, and their rooms should be free, even if the maid could not be removed.

After speaking with Roberta, Margaret called her friend, society columnist Poppy Dill. Poppy knew everybody from West Coast to East, and all the choicest spots in between. If anyone knew about Big Ed and Lucia Rose, Poppy would.

"Big Ed Grant? Of course I know of him, although I haven't had the pleasure of meeting him in person. I met his late wife, Gracie, years ago when I still went out and about. She was killed by a horse, of all things. Nasty brutes." Poppy was notorious for her reluctance—indeed refusal—to leave her apartment, where she composed her "Social Scene" column a few days a week for one of the city tabloid newspapers. She claimed that actually meeting the social figures and celebrities she dished the dirt about influenced her impartiality. Many claimed she didn't go out because nobody was really important enough for her to waste money on expensive clothes, and besides, too many people would like to shoot her for some of the items she printed about them.

"Big Ed used to meddle in politics quite a bit. He was probably delighted when the Bush boy got elected governor of Texas instead of that divine woman. He's got plenty of money, but I haven't heard much about him in ages. There's that girl of his, though. Tales about her manage to drift up here from time to time."

Margaret wasn't at all surprised that Poppy had heard rumors of little Lucy.

"Tell me about her."

"Lucia Rose? There's not all that much to tell. She didn't fit in at home, so she went to school in Massachusetts. Not one of the important schools like Harvard or Smith or Wellsley. Perhaps it was Boston University or the like. Anyhow, I understand that she got caught up in all those liberal ideas they spout off up there, and that didn't please her daddy one bit, so he had to bring her home.

"When he went to round her up, she simply disappeared for several months and he practically had the FBI searching for her. Claimed she'd been kidnapped. He even had a ransom note to show. Ha! It was a fake. She'd run off with some long-haired revolutionary environmentalist she met in Boston. He came from a good family, though. Related to the Cabots or the Lowells, I seem to recall. They finally found the two of them hugging trees in New Hampshire. They had hoped to collect the ransom to save some sort of wildlife." From Poppy's tone, it was clear that survival of downtrodden species was nothing she approved of. "Big Ed hauled her back to Texas, and put her under the guidance of Carolyn Sue again, since Gracie was long dead. I wonder if that was wise. Not that I'm saying anything against Carolyn Sue, but that marriage to Prince Aldo can't have made her the best mentor for a young girl."

"Well, little Lucy Rose has convinced Carolyn Sue that the only place for her is in New York, and apparently her father has agreed to let her come. She's arriving the day after tomorrow, staying with me for a while, and interviewing for a personal assistant job with Roberta Reeves the day after."

"Roberta could use some assisting," Poppy said, "not that I'm saying a word against her, either, but she never returns calls; she never gets her committee things done on time. I always expect to be writing up a disaster instead of a triumph when Roberta is in charge. You'll have to bring Lucy around to visit with me one day soon. I'd like to see how she's turned out."

"Not blond," Margaret said.

"That's a pity," Poppy said almost sadly. "Well, it probably matters in Dallas, but it won't matter quite so much in New York. We have all those Latinas and so many Asian girls on the streets. With all that dark hair around, very likely nobody will notice."

While Poppy shared some minor gossip about minor social personages, Margaret's thoughts were elsewhere. She hoped Lucy Rose wouldn't take it into her head to elope again with some environmentally conscious lad met on the streets of Manhattan, or decide to organize a protest on behalf of all the dark-haired Latinos in the city. Big Ed sounded as though he wouldn't take kindly to the idea, nor would Carolyn Sue. Maybe Paul had been right to warn her to be afraid.

"Do you think I've taken on too much trouble?" Margaret asked.

Poppy thought for a moment. "Probably not you." But she wouldn't elaborate. Instead she asked about Paul and his plans to marry the Honourable Georgina. "That's a wedding I might well leave my home to attend," she said. "Carolyn Sue will do a grand job. I can almost see it now. The music, the candles, the flowers . . ."

"I believe Georgina has put her foot down there. She definitely doesn't want to be orchestrated by Carolyn Sue. She has very firm ideas about a lovely simple country wedding, if they decide to go ahead and finally marry."

"You English girls." Poppy sniffed. "You don't know the first thing about glamour. Carolyn Sue was born with the Big Picture firmly in mind, and she knows how to throw a party. That big old house of hers will be perfect." Not that Poppy had ever visited Carolyn Sue's big old house, and it wasn't at all old. Just a sprawling mass of pale yellow brick that went on for acres and acres. Carolyn Sue loved showing pictures of new wings added and facades redone, the room that had been transformed into a gigantic closet, the new white upholstery in her all-white drawing room.

"Georgina will surely want to be married in England, or at the very least, at her house in the Caribbean, where she and Paul met," Margaret said. "I think the Caribbean house would be lovely for a wedding."

"I couldn't possibly fly to England or the Caribbean," Poppy said. "It's much too far. At least Texas is right here in my own country, and Carolyn Sue would know how to make me feel at home. I remember from the old days how damp England can be, and I am not cut out for tropical heat. It will be in Texas." She was so firm that Margaret almost believed her.

"We'll see," Margaret said. She tried not to imagine a contest of wills between Carolyn Sue and her future daughter-in-law. And she wasn't yet convinced that Paul and Georgina would ever marry. Well, that wasn't her concern at the moment.

"There's the matter of Doctor Dale," Poppy said suddenly.

"In what respect?"

"He's very concerned about the environment. He told me so himself."

Margaret's silence must have sounded like disbelief, because Poppy added, "Even I must visit a dentist from time to time, and he happened to mention his very deep concern about the rain forests in South America. Well, I'd hate to see Lucy Rose get involved in some wild scheme of his. He was talking about making a pilgrimage to the Amazon before everything is all gone."

"I hadn't known about his environmental concerns, but he's old enough to be Lucy's father," Margaret said. "I know what people say about him and women, but isn't he still firmly extramaritally attached to some woman?"

"Oh, Lorna, yes. It's been an open secret for years and years. I don't know how Roberta has put up with it for so long. I suppose it frees her to do as she pleases. But mark my words, there'll be a big breakup someday, probably when Dale has enough of Roberta's own extracurricular activities. He's so busy with his practice, and Roberta has so many obligations of her own, that I doubt they meet more than once a week, if that."

"Wasn't Richard Centner, the real estate man, what pleased Roberta at one time?"

"You heard about that? Well, of course you'd hear. It's common knowledge on the street." As if Poppy and the street—any street—had even a nodding acquaintance. "Don't worry about it. It was just a fling and it's long over. He wasn't quite . . . right for someone as prominent as Roberta Reeves. There was that bit of scandal at the time of the decorator show house you were involved in and his name got mentioned quite a bit because he and Peter Anton owned the building where the murder took place. Roberta likes to keep herself scandal-free. At least Dale has the decency to keep Lorna in the background. Not that Lorna isn't in the spotlight in her own right. She's taken a rather high-profile job as an editor at one of those fashion magazines that keep trying to crush *Vogue* and *Harper's Bazaar*. I heard that Tina Brown talked to her about working at her new magazine, but Lorna took the other job. Now, do keep me posted on the girl's progress. Working for Roberta seems like a harmless enough occupation for a young woman, although I would have thought she would be aiming at the magazine business. Most young things seem to find editing the height of glamour. If only they knew how hard we journalists work to produce our copy."

Margaret suppressed a smile at the picture of Poppy at work. Typically she sat in her boudoir in a lacy robe and typed slowly on the keyboard of the computer her newspaper insisted she use in lieu of the ancient typewriter to which she was accustomed. She didn't even have to venture out to find her items. A bevy of fawning friends gathered tidbits and fed them to her to fill the column.

Then Poppy added, "Maybe if the girl plays her cards right, she can persuade Dale to introduce her to Lorna. She could start out as an editorial assistant and end up dictating to all you poor things what the length of your skirts should be and what makeup is in for next season."

With that, Poppy decided that she needed to work on her next column, probably an item mentioning the arrival of the wealthy, desirable Lucia Rose Grant in the midst of New York society.

Poppy would help set Lucy on her way to social stardom, since a favorable mention in "Social Scene" invariably attracted invitations to high-profile social events, and invitations led to introductions to the kind of young men little Lucy needed to know to find herself a suitable mate from New York social elevated circles. Certainly, the highest New York social circles did not include dangerous Latino boys, so Margaret wouldn't have to worry

that she'd take up with someone unsuitable. She'd have
to do that on her own.

It was going to work out nicely after all.

Chapter 5

Feeling that she'd done what she could to prepare for Lucy's arrival, Margaret idled for a day, reading her art history book, and was interrupted only by one more call from Carolyn Sue.

"Everything's movin' along," she said. "I talked to Lucy Rose, and she promised she'd be good as gold while she's up there. She's real eager to find a nice woman to work for, and she'll be a treasure. That girl is ready to take on any challenge."

Margaret decided against mentioning the interview with Roberta. Since Carolyn Sue certainly knew her, she didn't want her calling Roberta to press her to hire Lucy. If the girl was any good at all, she'd have to make a favorable impression on her own. All she said was, "I have some leads for possible jobs. Nothing definite."

"Well, that's just fine," Carolyn Sue said. "It'll be a great relief to me and to Big Ed to see the girl settled."

"The thing is, I'm not sure that anything I've lined up will come with living space. I worry that Lucy won't be comfortable here with me for long." Nor would Margaret be comfortable with a perpetual apartment guest.

"Let me just think a minute. I'm leaving San Francisco tomorrow, and will be back home by the afternoon.

I'll give a call to my rental agent up there in New York and see what he has available that would be comfortable and safe. Housing is tight in Manhattan just now, and I wouldn't want little Lucy livin' in some . . . dangerous neighborhood. I owe that much to her precious momma."

Margaret wondered if in addition to the rather grand apartment buildings Carolyn Sue had acquired in Chelsea, she had also ventured into the world of slum landlords, with buildings in "dangerous neighborhoods." Probably not in most people's view, but Carolyn Sue viewed even the Upper West Side of Manhattan as undesirable, and thought that Greenwich Village was one step above Hell. She did approve of Chelsea, though, probably because the peaceful, dog-walking, largely gay community there was always reasonably well groomed and well dressed. Not dangerous.

"I'd appreciate your help," Margaret said. "I wouldn't know where to begin searching for an apartment for her."

"I'll be in touch, soon as I have a chance to send out feelers."

Margaret ventured out in the afternoon to her local Gristede's to lay in a supply of groceries to keep Lucy Rose in Diet Cokes and healthy snacks. There was always a chance, given her environmentalist leanings, that she was a vegetarian. That would probably be considered the greatest sin of all in Texas, which was overrun by large cattle in their pre-rare/medium-rare Sirloin state. She definitely hoped that Lucy wasn't accustomed to home-cooked gourmet meals. Margaret was a good enough cook, but she preferred to cook on alternate days, certainly not every day. Or maybe cooking was one of Lucy's talents. That would be nice. Carolyn Sue was always talking about traditional and delicious all-white-meat chicken salad in a way that indicated it was the basis of the national cuisine of the southern states. Ah well, there was always Chinese takeout.

She called a car service and arranged to have a Town Car meet Lucy's plane and bring her into Manhattan. Now there was nothing to do but wait.

Sam De Vere called her in the evening to apologize for being absent from her life for some days.

"I was wondering if you'd been damaged by a violent felon," Margaret said, knowing full well that De Vere was currently engaged in investigating white-collar crime. Still, some of those well-barbered executives kept pretty sharp letter openers in their desks, and everybody seemed to have a gun these days.

"Nothing so exciting," he said. "My father and I went up to the Connecticut coast to go fishing in Long Island Sound. Didn't Paul tell you?" She admitted that Paul had neglected to do so. "The bluefish were running in the Sound, and I don't see enough of Pop these days. He's bored out there in New Jersey, so we went up to the town where the family used to vacation when I was a kid. He keeps in touch with some of the old-timers with boats, so we went for the blues."

"Catch any?"

"Baskets. They were practically jumping into the boat. I could bring some fillets around tomorrow night for a cozy dinner. Just the two of us. I even brought back some of the last of the sweet corn."

"Alas, I'm expecting a house guest tomorrow for a few days," Margaret said, briefly resenting Lucy's imminent arrival. "Can you freeze it so I can cook it after she's gone?" Then she told him about doing the little favor for Carolyn Sue. De Vere was extremely fond of Paul's mother, so he agreed that any favor she asked should be promptly accommodated.

"Carolyn Sue's a hell of a gal," he said. "Is this kid going to be hanging out at your place for long?" That pleased Margaret, the idea that he didn't want an outsider interfering in their privacy.

"I hope not," Margaret said. "I'm hoping she'll burrow into the life of whoever hires her, and she won't be my responsibility any longer."

"Miss . . . ? Lady . . . ?" The girl at Margaret's door the next afternoon was backed by an enormous pile of luggage. She was definitely not blond, and it would have been a terrible mistake if she'd tried to be. She had a thatch of lush, dark, almost black hair, thick dark brows, and piercing greenish eyes fringed with dark lashes. She was of medium height, slim, and tanned. She was absolutely and uniquely stunning, nothing like any of the pretty young things who filled the junior charity committee rosters, and especially nothing like the multicolored hair, pierced-body-parts girls who constituted the denizens of the New York club scene, of which Margaret knew only because the press liked to do feature stories about club kids, or about nefarious happenings at the various venues. On looks alone, Lucia Rose would set Manhattan to breathing heavily.

"Come in. You must be Lucy Rose. Please call me Margaret. I don't fuss about titles here in America, except when they can be used to get you a better table in a restaurant. I'll help you with your things."

"Oh, please don't trouble yourself. There's a nice man from your building who brought up my things, and he said he'd be right back to help me get them inside. Ah, there he is. José, honey. If you could just bring these suitcases into the apartment."

José, a usually solemn, young handyman, beamed at little Lucy, and Margaret even caught a hint of adoration in his look. Then she remembered Paul's comment about Lucy and the Latinos, and hoped she wouldn't end up prying Lucy from the arms of a hard-working and, incidentally, very much married José. He was always telling her about how well his kids were doing in school.

After hauling half a dozen suitcases into the apartment, he loitered in the foyer, still gazing at Lucy, until Margaret said firmly, "Thank you so much, José. You've been very helpful." But before she could find a couple of dollars to tip him for his trouble, Lucy had whipped out a five and handed it to him with a glowing smile.

"I hope I'll be seeing you soon, José," Lucy said. "You're so kind. And so strong."

José departed looking very much like a man who had been whacked by a log.

Lucy sighed. "It's almost too easy," she said.

"Come along to your room so you can get settled," Margaret said. "I'm afraid it's terribly small, but Carolyn Sue is looking into an apartment for you, so this is just temporary. And you have an interview with Mrs. Reeves tomorrow about a possible job as her assistant. If that kind of work doesn't suit you, I've made some inquiries about you working with some interior designer friends."

"Goodness, I don't know a thing about interior design."

"There's nothing to know. But I think Roberta Reeves might be a better choice, just to get started in New York."

"It sounds fine," Lucy said. "Although when I was at college in Boston, I used to think that it would be fun to be in publishing, you know, as an editor. You get to pick out articles and stories that will help make the world a better place, and like that. A lot of my college friends went to New York to work in publishing."

"Maybe after you get a little experience with Mrs. Reeves, you'll have a chance to look them up and look around for something else. Here's your room."

"Yes, it is small," Lucy said as she took in the guest bedroom. "I don't know where I'll put all my clothes." Suddenly she sounded like a pathetic little girl who needed to be looked after. "I mean, I can't just leave them in the suitcases."

"You can share my closet," Margaret said reluctantly. "I don't have a lot of clothes." That wasn't entirely true, but she hadn't put away her summer clothes yet. She could store the summer frocks in boxes and make room in the closet for Lucy. Then she thought, Why did I give in so easily? I don't want to share my closet space with this girl. Not even for a few days. She hoped most of all that Lucy wouldn't suggest that she take over Margaret's much larger bedroom. Proper hospitality, after all, could only go just so far.

"I suppose sharing would be okay," Lucy said. She did have a sweet smile.

So she spent the rest of the day putting away clothes in the dresser and running back and forth to Margaret's closet with what appeared to be a very fine selection of dresses and neat little suits, even a couple of evening gowns. She hung some garments on the hooks in her own room, and lined up an impressive array of shoes along the wall at the side of the room.

Margaret decided not to hint that if Roberta Reeves hired her, she might also provide a room in the Reeves' apartment. That would be asking almost too much.

They dined out that evening at the little French neighborhood restaurant where Margaret and De Vere often ate. Lucy displayed a startling command of French, which appeared to please Hervé, the waiter with the sexy eyes. Those eyes remained fastened on Lucy throughout the meal. The girl had a real gift. It was almost as if Hervé's old friend Margaret didn't exist. His loyal customer as well, Margaret thought grumpily.

"You speak French well," Margaret said.

"I studied it at college, and then my father sent me to Europe one summer, and I spent a couple of months outside of Paris. I pick up languages easily. French, Spanish, and I don't know what all."

"You must be tired after your flight," Margaret said as she scooped up the last of her apple tart. "We can stroll back to the apartment to get some fresh air and then . . ."

"Isn't there someplace else we can go now?" Lucy asked. "It's New York, after all, and isn't this the city that never sleeps?"

"I'm afraid that I sleep, even if the city doesn't. Perhaps you could ring Paul Castrocani and see if he's up for a night on the town."

Lucy sniffed. "He's such a baby. And I know he disapproves of me."

The latter might be true, but Paul was hardly a baby. Margaret thought for a moment. At least Paul didn't appear to have succumbed to Lucy's enchantments the way the other men who had encountered her had. Was it her unique look or something else that attracted them? Margaret shrugged mentally. Definitely a gift, but unfathomable to Margaret. Probably just as well that De Vere hadn't turned up tonight. She'd lost half her closet, no point in losing the only man who interested her in the least.

"Maybe I'll just take a taxi down to Greenwich Village," Lucy said. "Or go to one of those clubs they're always writing about in *People* or talking about on television."

"I wouldn't feel right about letting you wander around by yourself," Margaret said. "I promised Carolyn Sue I'd look after you, at least for the first few days of your visit."

"I'm not visiting," Lucy said firmly. "This is my new life. I'll be all right. I'm careful, and I can always find somebody who'll take care of me."

I'll just bet you can, Margaret thought. And when they stood up to leave, with Lucy apparently agreeable to an early night, Hervé nearly dropped a tray as he lunged across the room to help Lucy from her chair, pick up her handbag from the floor, and guide her to the coatroom to retrieve her jacket.

"*Merci,*" she said graciously, and Hervé melted.

"Return to us soon, mademoiselle," he managed to say breathlessly.

"Too easy," Lucy murmured as they stepped into the cool night. They walked in silence for a couple of blocks, but when they stopped at a red light at a cross street, Lucy suddenly flagged down a cruising taxi and was into the cab and away before Margaret grasped what was happening.

She felt a tiny touch of annoyance at the girl's behavior, then she shrugged it away. Lucy would certainly find someone to take care of her, and Margaret needn't worry. It was only when she was at home and ready for bed that she realized she hadn't given Lucy a key to the apartment. It was nearly two in the morning when she was awakened by the doorbell and shuffled out to the foyer to let Lucy in.

"I had *such* a great time. I met some terrific people at this club I went to, and someone even said that Leonardo DiCaprio was upstairs in the VIP room. Tyler Anne will be so jealous when I tell her. She's my best friend in Dallas."

Margaret yawned. "Did you get to meet him?"

Lucy shook her head sadly. "They said he was with his posse, and nobody was allowed to bother them. But I'll meet him someday, you wait. I did see some models I recognized from the magazines. You know, they're not so gorgeous in person, really kind of plain, no makeup, and they don't dress well at all. And," she added, "they don't seem to be very smart. But there were some really cool guys I talked to and I'm going to see them again. They say they're around the clubs every night practically. They were really interesting. They know all the fun clubs to go to and who the best DJs are, and where the celebrities like to hang out. One of them, Frankie Martinez, has this big, fast sports car, so he and a couple of others drove me home tonight." Lucy was clearly high on her evening, although Margaret happily didn't detect that she was high on anything else.

"Don't you think New York is beautiful at night? In Dallas, all the buildings look the same, glass towers, Mexican restaurants and steak houses. I'm going to love it here." Lucy seemed thrilled to be there, and Margaret felt strangely pleased.

"Time to hit the hay," Lucy said, and yawned. "I want

to be in good shape for my interview." She stopped at the door to her room. "You know, if I'm going to be staying here, it might be a good idea if you gave me a key. That way I wouldn't have to wake you up to let me in when I came home.

"I mean, I might be working late with Mrs. Reeves or something, or if she gives me a rush job to finish, or maybe I'll have to attend one of her charity parties to make sure everything goes okay. So a key would be good to have."

"Already thought of it. Consider it done," Margaret said. "Good night." She closed the door to her room. The key would be done tomorrow, anyhow. Then she thought, but don't consider this home. Not a chance of that.

Chapter 6

"*Mrs. Reeves is* a very prominent socialite," Margaret told little Lucy in the morning. Thanks to her grocery shopping, there was something to give her guest for breakfast. Lucy claimed, in any case, to prefer juice and coffee to bacon and eggs and freshly baked croissants. That was fortunate, because none of those were available. "She's active on many different committees that organize charity events, so she has a lot of paperwork and tasks to keep in order. Carolyn Sue thought working with someone like her would teach you a few things about the way society works here. Her committee ladies are also socially prominent women, and I should say that they can be quite demanding, but they are basically quite nice to work with."

"I can handle that stuff," Lucy said. "It's all a matter of being organized, and keeping lists of things to be done and when. I used to have to keep track of all kinds of things for my father when he was organizing political campaigns, raising funds for his candidates, throwing parties to get people to give money in the first place. Nothing to it. I'll pick up on where to get things and who to call to get things done. No problem. You can probably find anything you want in New York. It's not that easy in

Dallas to find everything you need, even if the people at Neiman's are real helpful. Of course, almost everybody knows my father, and they like to keep on his good side, so they used to go out of their way to get me what I wanted. I can handle Mrs. Reeves' problems."

Little Lucy Rose wore a simple dark green suit with a not-too-short skirt and matching pumps and handbag. Carolyn Sue was always firm in her belief that handbags and shoes must match. Maybe it was a Texas thing. In any event, Carolyn Sue would be proud of her. She wore plain gold earrings and a gold pin on her lapel. Perfectly ladylike and proper for both the season and the occasion. Roberta would notice the details, and Margaret was certain she would approve.

"I think you shouldn't mention too much that you've only worked for your father, taking care of his social obligations," Margaret said. "What I mean is, talk about taking care of things, but don't emphasize that it was a family thing. You really haven't had much experience in the greater world outside your home."

Lucy tossed her head, as if to say, You don't know how much experience I've had. How lucky to have hair that didn't disarrange itself every time it was shaken, Margaret thought. In Lucy's case, it just fell back into place. "I did a lot of work with protest groups when I was at college in Boston," she said. "And then again when I went back home to Dallas. Daddy didn't approve, but I think it helped get his candidates some votes. The Mexicans aren't all aliens; a lot of them are citizens and can vote just like us. Besides, they liked me. Carolyn Sue's friends thought I was crazy; I suppose Carolyn Sue disapproved as much as Daddy did, but"—she tossed her obedient hair again—"who cares what people think."

The morning dragged on. Lucy wanted to do some shopping, but Margaret didn't want to risk losing her to the streets of Manhattan before the two o'clock appointment with Roberta. But Lucy was restless, as though she had to swallow the whole wide world of New York in one gulp, right now.

"You'll have plenty of time to see the sights, the shops, the people," Margaret said. "I think you should make some notes on what you plan to say to Roberta, what you know how to do, the kind of experience you've actually had. But do avoid the protests and the union organizing. I'm not at all sure that Mrs. Reeves has the slightest interest in the lives of Mexicans or the state of the union movement." Or anything or anybody who wasn't an upper-class white person who could somehow enhance her position in society.

"How about the environment?" Lucy asked, and Margaret wondered if she was about to detail her disappearance into the woods with the Boston youth of good family.

"I suppose she's as interested as the ordinary person. I've never heard of her running a committee to benefit an endangered species or to promote wildflowers. I understand Doctor Reeves has some environmental interests, though. Rain forests, I believe."

"I like that kind of stuff. I did some things to help the environment when I was at school in Boston." But she left it there. No sordid escapades were revealed. With a sudden shift of topic, she asked, "Why are you a lady? Is your father, like, a prince or something, like Paul's?"

"My father, now deceased, was the Earl of Brayfield, a title my brother, David, now holds. And earl's daughters have the honorary title of lady. It doesn't mean much.

There are earls and viscounts and ladies all over the place in England. It means something to my brother because he now owns our family home, Priam's Priory, which is a very old Tudor house with important history. It used to house a religious community. And it even has a couple of ghosts."

"Really? You must be kidding. Ghosts aren't real."

"Ours are. I'll tell you about them one day. I've actually seen them both. They even got themselves mixed up in a murder a few years back."

Margaret could be glad that taking charge of Lucy, in a manner of speaking, did not entail a murder for once. For an ordinary person, she'd encountered far too many violent deaths, and she certainly didn't care to come upon another.

"Still don't believe in them," Lucy said. "I'd have to see them for myself."

"Perhaps you'll visit England one day, and you can stop at Priam's Priory, although the ghosts don't materialize on demand. Still, you never know when they will be discovered walking the halls."

Lucy still didn't look convinced of their reality, but Margaret was pleased by her offer to wash the few cups and glasses from breakfast. At least she wasn't above doing simple domestic chores.

Finally, it was time to head off to Roberta Reeves' apartment, conveniently located on Park Avenue. Lucy agreed to walk, since the day was fine and much warmer than previously. When they reached Park, Lucy looked down the double roadway, toward the gold-capped Helmsley Building, and sniffed. "Boring street, don't you think?"

"One of the best neighborhoods," Margaret said, "and by 'best' I mean most expensive. In the spring, the center strip is planted with lovely flowers, and there are lighted Christmas trees all the length of Park at holiday time. I don't think I'd care to live here myself. I'd miss the delis and the Korean fruit stands and little restaurants around where I live."

"I'd like to live in Greenwich Village," Lucy said. "I only caught a glimpse of it last night when Frankie drove around there, but—"

Margaret interrupted. "About last night. I really don't like to have you running off that way. At least not until you're more accustomed to the city. And I wonder if you should just take up with any boy who happens along. What would Carolyn Sue say if she knew?"

"She's not my mother," Lucy said reasonably. "Not even my father dares to tell me what to do."

"I suppose not, but I'd really prefer it if you would use some common sense, and listen to what I say. I'm not trying to keep you away from fun, but I do have reasons for giving you gentle warnings. Promise?"

"I promise to listen," Lucy said, "but I won't promise not to make my own choices."

That would have to suffice. They were approaching the bland, gray-white pile of a building where Dr. and Mrs. Dale Reeves resided. Margaret had only been once to their apartment, but as they entered through the heavy door, opened by the requisite stern doorman in uniform, she remembered the elaborate lobby. The doorman took their names and announced them by calling upstairs. "You are expected," he said, and pointed them toward the elevators. The elevators were as baroque as the lobby, and opened directly into the foyer of the Reeves' apartment. Black-and-white marble squares like a giant checkerboard provided the floor treatment. Gilt mirrors reflected the two women. To Margaret's eyes, the sameness of the New York apartments of the wealthy was far more boring than the uncluttered stretch of Park Avenue. Roberta had acquired two apartments, or maybe three, and had knocked them all together to create far too much space for only two people.

There was a uniformed maid to greet them and usher them into a spacious but old-fashioned-looking and densely cluttered drawing room, which Roberta Reeves clearly used as her office. Giovanni would love to get his hands on this place and dispose of all this stodgy furniture, Margaret thought, but that would probably have to wait until one or the other of the Reeveses decided to embark on another marital adventure. Second or third wives were notorious for enjoying the process of erasing traces of former spouses, and that was best accomplished by frantic redecorating.

Margaret was surprised to find that Roberta was actually awaiting them, instead of making a grand entrance some minutes after they were seated. The tables in the room were piled with manila folders, yellow lined pads, jars of pens and pencils, boxes of envelopes ready to be addressed, all the stuff of a committee chairwoman.

After dutifully serving on numerous committees, Margaret was familiar with all of it, and goodness knew, she never wanted to address another envelope again. Still, she had mastered a beautiful italic handwriting, and therefore was much in demand as the chief address inscriber.

Roberta greeted her with careful air kisses. She had obviously just had her hair done and didn't want to risk moving a hair out of place. The threads of gray that Margaret remembered and had thought quite distinguished had been artfully colored. Roberta hadn't kept her figure, and was in fact rather solid looking, but she had a nice face and lovely straight white teeth, thanks probably to Dr. Dale.

"Lovely to see you, Roberta," Margaret said. "May I present Lucia Rose Grant from Dallas, the young woman I mentioned."

"Hello, Miss Grant. You must find New York quite a change from Texas. And you're looking well, Margaret," Roberta said. "I don't believe I've seen you since that tragic show house thing you worked on." She was taking a close look at Lucy as she made small talk with Margaret. From her expression, it was clear that Roberta was as struck by Lucy's unusual looks as Margaret had been. "Let's sit down and chat a bit, Miss Grant, shall we?"

They sat. The maid wheeled in a tea tray with a massive and impressive silver Georgian tea set, and fragile porcelain cups and saucers. There were tiny sandwiches, as well, and a plate of pastries.

"I hope it's not too early for tea, Margaret. I assure you that Mrs. Frost, my cook, has had strict training in the proper brewing of tea, so you won't be disappointed. Now, Miss Grant . . ."

"Please call me Lucy, Mrs. Reeves. Miss Grant sounds so old."

"As does Mrs. Reeves. I'm just Roberta. Now, Margaret has persuaded me that I could use an assistant and that you'd be ideal for the job."

"I think I could handle it," Lucy said. "I'm very organized, and I've spent a lot of my life arranging complicated events for my father. He was a state senator, you know, and after he retired from active politics, he entertained a good deal, and of course did a lot of fund-raising."

"Your mother . . . ?"

"My mother died when I was a teenager. I told her that mare was a killer, but she wouldn't listen to me. She had to make her own choices. I guess I'm like her in that, but I know the difference between a dangerous horse and merely a lively one. She grew up in Texas, but her people came from Virginia," she added, as if that would explain her mother's tragic ignorance of horses.

"I see." Roberta Reeves wasn't at all interested in horses, but Margaret was wondering, What are you, Lucy Rose—a lively one, or a dangerous one?

"I think my work is a bit different from your father's," Roberta was saying. "The people I deal with are very fine people, socially prominent, and financially comfortable."

"We have some fine people in Texas," Lucy said, almost pertly, "and many of them are financially comfortable, or just plain rich, as we like to say back home. As for social prominence, isn't that how others define it? I mean, it's not something you can put on, like a coat. It's more like the coat other people imagine you're wearing."

Roberta smiled coldly. "She's got a brain, I'll say that. But can she manage my affairs?"

"Mrs. Reeves, you're just the kind of person I want to be. Beautiful and confident, friends with all the right people. I'll bet you don't have to deal with a lot of politicians, either."

Roberta seemed pleased by the flattery. "Oh, we generally invite the mayor and the governor to our little affairs, even though they don't get along all that well. But I try to keep politics in the background. It makes people so cross, and I like our events to be happy ones."

"You must have to seat the mayor and governor at separate tables that both look equally important so neither is offended. That's important. I've had to work hard on seating arrangements so that you don't end up with a table full of enemies. It keeps the shooting to a minimum."

Roberta looked briefly startled. "I don't recall any shooting incidents at any of our benefits. Does it happen often in Texas?"

"Often enough," Lucy said gaily. Then she added, "But I'm teasing. I was just imagining the mayor of New York taking out a revolver and shooting the governor of the state because he was seated at a better table."

Margaret suppressed a chuckle, but Roberta laughed out loud. "She's a charming girl, Margaret. Well, Miss Lucy, would you like to give it a try? I work long hours, from early in the morning until late at night. My husband is a very important dentist, so he doesn't spend much time at home, and it would be nice to have a young friend around."

"Oh yes, Mrs. Reeves . . . Roberta, I'd love to have the chance to work with you. And I don't mind long hours at all."

"I have to be out at meetings quite a bit, so you'll have to learn to handle crises on your own."

Lucy glanced at Margaret as if to say, Piece of cake.

"Where are you staying in New York, dear?" Roberta asked.

"I'm with Margaret for the moment, but I hope to find a place of my own soon. I'll try to find something that's close to here, so I can be available at a moment's notice." Margaret decided not to bring up the matter of Lucy actually staying at the Reeves' apartment. If it occurred to Roberta, all to the good. If it didn't, she would park Lucy someplace convenient. Surely there were places to rent on the East Side, even if they weren't part of Carolyn Sue's real estate empire.

And so it was settled. Lucy would begin work the next day. Roberta would provide lunch and occasional dinners, "especially when Dale can't make it home and I have no engagements."

"Until tomorrow, then," Lucy said. "Thank you, Roberta. I promise to do my best for you."

"I'm sure we're going to be great friends. You'll like my daughter, Susan. She's married to a lovely man, no children yet, but I keep hoping for a grandchild soon." Roberta Reeves didn't look especially pleased about the prospect of grandparenthood. "Susan does manage to come around to visit her old mother often enough. She's a bit older than you are, but I know she'll be happy to guide you around the social pitfalls of New York. And there are pitfalls, I can assure you. Associating with the right people, being seen at the right places. Yes, Susan will be the ideal person to take charge of your New York education."

Back on the street, Lucy said in a perfect imitation of Roberta's cultured tones, " 'She'll be happy to guide you around the social pitfalls of New York.' What rubbish. I wonder if I'll be able to survive that la-di-da nonsense for long. I'm sure I won't be able to stand the ideal Susan for more than two minutes. And exactly how can one be a 'very important dentist'? A dentist is just a dentist, and you can't change him into something desirable."

Margaret didn't answer at first. Then she said, "Dale Reeves is certainly important, as dentists go, but I agree that it's a kind of flimsy importance. Probably Roberta needs to feel that he's important for her own self-esteem, and because he treats a lot of celebrities. He's even a kind of celebrity himself, showing up on television to talk about dentistry." And all the while she was speaking, she was calculating what she would have to do to persuade Giovanni to hire Lucy after she'd had enough of Roberta Reeves. She definitely did not want to spend her days in an endless job search for little Lucy Rose, or to be responsible in any way for this young woman for too long.

Chapter 7

The next day, Lucia Rose dove into her seemingly endless array of costumes suitable for attending to a New York socialite, and departed early for work at Roberta's apartment. Margaret felt a bit as though she'd sent off a child to preschool, and was at last free to pursue her own interests, such as they were, for a brief, precious time.

There had been no further talk of seeking out a permanent place for Lucy to stay, so the girl was not leaving Margaret's place immediately. That was almost all right, and Lucy might even end up sharing a bit of Margaret's substantial rent. On the other hand, perhaps such a thing might not occur to a quite well-off young woman who had probably never had to pay the rent in her entire life. Then there were the groceries and the dinners out, the laundry, and the housekeeping details. Little Lucy was likely accustomed to having servants handle those mundane details of living, and while Margaret had a regular, although infrequent, cleaning woman who took care of the big jobs, she certainly was in no position to hire a full-time servant.

With that thought, she decided to have another cup of morning coffee, and remember fondly the old days at Priam's Priory, where her capable mother, the Countess of Brayfield, used to command a substantial staff and everything got done beautifully and regularly, so that by the time Margaret was a teenager, ready to go off to school in Switzerland, no commands were really necessary. Everyone knew his or her job, and her mother needed only to issue daily instructions to the cook and to alert the rest of the staff to the pending arrival of the frequent visitors who enjoyed the civilized society of the Priory.

Not for the first time did Margaret wish she were back in the comfort of her old home. But her brother, now the Earl, had taken over the place, and he was by nature incapable of closely supervising the details of life as her mother had been. The young women David took up with and thought of as prospective brides were not of the same class and had little experience in running a grand household, should David ever settle on one of them.

The village publican's daughter, for example, was an entirely jolly girl and very pretty, but she could not be expected to understand the basic necessities of the Priory's way of life, or even her brother's. Someone like little Lucy Rose would probably have a better handle on running a large household like Priam's Priory. Margaret shuddered. She would see to it that little Lucy and her brother never met. David was dopey about women, and as Lucy had noted about herself and men, it was "too easy" to bedazzle and enchant them.

In the meantime, Priam's Priory would stumble along on the efforts of the old servants her mother had trained, and who would stay on for life. None of them would dream of changing the established patterns, and Cook and the maids, the butler, and even the grooms in the stable and the farm laborers would stick with tradition rather than bend to David's whims. He knew his place as the master of the Priory, just as well as the servants knew theirs. The place would keep on going in the usual fashion through this generation at least.

Margaret had an appointment to have her hair done today. She'd let it go far too long. Surely someone she knew would be at Norman's "hair boutique," as he called it, and she could spend a few peaceful hours being cosseted, trimmed, and gilded while she picked up a few crumbs of gossip.

It was the kind of fall day that Margaret liked best: cool but not cold, with a clear blue sky and only a few puffy clouds. Her appointment with Norman was scheduled for eleven, so she would be in and out in time for lunch, unless some other preferred client had a coiffeur-related crisis that Norman had to handle personally.

The hair salon on the second floor of a brownstone on a cross street between Lexington and Third looked more like a pleasant drawing room than a professional business full of shiny hair dryers and stainless-steel sinks. The equipment was all there, but cleverly hidden by folding screens and potted plants. Norman had comfortable easy chairs under the dryers so that patrons could catch up on *Vogue* and *Harper's Bazaar* or chat in comfort as the hot air blew through their tresses, while elsewhere the inspired colorist worked her magic, transforming horrid gray hairs to youthful shades of blond and titian.

"Lady Margaret, my darling! How wonderful you look, even before I've gotten my hands on your hair." Norman brushed cheeks with Margaret. "I'll only be a minute while I finish up with Mrs. Cheever." Norman didn't look like anybody's idea of a high-priced hair designer. He was short and rather plump, with chipmunk cheeks and—unfortunate for a hair magician—not a hair on his own head. Audrey Cheever, with her damp page-boy hanging limply to her shoulders, gave Margaret a tiny wave, then scowled impatiently at Norman. How dare he waste her appointment time on someone else, even Lady Margaret Priam!

With Margaret settled in a puffy armchair to await her turn, Norman returned to Mrs. Cheever, whom Margaret had met all too frequently on the social circuit. A truly vicious gossip who liked to feed Poppy Dill sensational if inaccurate accounts of goings-on in her circle. Happily, Poppy was a seasoned enough newswoman to take it all with some skepticism, and always found someone to corroborate the tales before printing them in "Social Scene."

While Norman was cutting and combing, Mrs. Cheever squinted at the mirror to see the others in the salon who might be listening. Apparently no one of consequence, because she hissed in a rather loud whisper to Margaret's reflection, "Margaret, we must talk about what Roberta Reeves is up to."

Startled, Margaret raised her eyes from a thick, thick copy of *W*, and smiled blankly. If Roberta was up to something other than what she already knew about—namely, little Lucy—it might be wise to hear Audrey out. She wasn't always misinformed and incorrect; it was just that she embroidered the details with abandon.

"I'll tell all while I'm drying," Audrey said. Norman turned her around so her back was to the mirror and she faced Margaret. He finished cutting, and rolled her hair into big rollers. "Put me next to Margaret," she said, "so we can talk."

Norman said, "I'll put you two together after I've finished with her. Can't stop the production line for mere gossip."

The girl who washed her hair was gentle, and Margaret got a good deal of sensual pleasure from the experience. Norman trimmed and styled her hair—authentically blond, to the envy of too many to count, who had to make do with a shade from a box—and directed her to a dryer next to Audrey Cheever, who, Margaret noticed, could barely contain her eagerness to regale her with a tale of Roberta Reeves' behavior, or misbehavior, depending on the closeness of one's friendship with her.

"Roberta has hired an assistant!" Audrey said. "She told Terry Thompson, who's on a committee with me, and Terry told me."

"I'd heard something . . ." Margaret decided to find out why this was such juicy gossip before she admitted her part in the matter.

"They're saying she hired her not so much to help out with all those committee affairs she manages so badly, but to break up Dale's thing with Lorna. They say the girl is absolutely fabulous. Gorgeous. I guess Roberta just got sick and tired of everybody talking about Dale and Lorna and decided to do something about it. She probably figured she could handle a sweet young thing, and once it got going, she could get rid of her. Lorna is going to be furious. Can you imagine it?"

"No, I can't imagine it at all," Margaret said shortly, and hoped that little Lucy had her wits about her, or at least enough wits not to be tossed out on the Aubusson like a staked goat to attract a tiger or two. It was a distasteful thought, but not really a scandal. If true, it seemed a shabby way for a wife to treat a husband, but perhaps Roberta felt desperate measures were in order. And again, if true, Roberta may have made a mistake in selecting Lucia Rose for the task.

"I hear that Carolyn Sue Hoopes found the girl and sent her to Roberta personally."

"Actually, it was me," Margaret said. "I mean, Carolyn Sue asked me to help find a job for a young friend of hers as a social secretary. Roberta hadn't thought about hiring an assistant and didn't know a thing about Lucia Rose until I brought her around. There was certainly no plan hatched to use her against Lorna and break up her relationship with Dale Reeves. So you're wrong about that. And Lucia Rose is staying with me for the present. She's a very pleasant young woman. Very young."

"Ah . . ." Audrey Cheever managed to look a bit chagrined. "I wouldn't have mentioned what people were saying had I known. I mean, you and Carolyn Sue and all . . ."

"I'm sure you wouldn't have said a thing," Margaret said. "Don't worry, dear. Lucy seems to have a sensible head on her shoulders, and since it was my idea, not Roberta's, she really can't have been planning to cast Lucy in her husband's direction. But it will make the girl's way smoother if you don't repeat the gossip. She's going to be meeting all the ladies in your set, and it wouldn't do for them to have nasty preconceived ideas about her role in the Reeves' establishment, now would it?"

"You're right," Audrey mumbled, and suddenly became intent on inspecting her nails. "I won't say another word. Norman! Aren't I dry yet?" She raised her voice to attract his attention. "I'm going to need to leave at once if I'm to get to my manicurist in time for my appointment."

Margaret concentrated on her magazine until it was time for her comb-out, trying not to believe that Roberta might actually have planned to find some sweet young thing to entice her husband away from his longtime mistress. Stranger things had happened, but the Roberta/Dale/Lorna triangle—or possibly rectangle if one counted in Richard Centner—had been going on for a long time, according to those who knew. What point was there in capsizing the boat now?

Audrey was already in another chair being fussed over by one of Norman's assistants, while Norman himself took care of Margaret. Another perk that came with having a title, she supposed.

"Looks terrific, Norman," Margaret said as she admired the simple, clean lines of her newly refurbished hair. "As always."

"It's always a pleasure to do your hair," Norman said. "What sort of poison is Mrs. Cheever sharing today?" Naturally, he'd want to know the latest gossip so he could shrug it off as old news when his clients started chattering about it.

"Some foolishness," Margaret said. "Entirely untrue, as I know for a fact."

"About par for the Cheever course," Norman said as he rearranged a single strand of hair to a place more to his liking. "Nothing you can repeat?"

"Nothing at all," Margaret said firmly. "Ah, Norman. I have a young friend from Texas staying with me, a protégé of Carolyn Sue Hoopes. I know you're awfully busy and mostly booked, but I wonder . . ."

"I'll fit her in if it's at all possible, for your sake," Norman said.

And Carolyn Sue's as well, Margaret thought. Sometimes piles of money were better than a title.

"I've often done Mrs. Hoopes' hair when she's in the city. Extraordinary what those Dallas ladies prefer. Big state, big money, and really big hair. Not to my taste, but the customer must be kept happy, even if she's not right."

"Norman, do you hear much gossip about Roberta Reeves? I don't want to know anything," she added quickly. "Just wondering if people talk about her."

Norman sighed. "Her name comes up. She's made herself so powerful that the other ladies are naturally a bit envious. I think they'd like to see her stumble. And there's idle gossip about the rest of the family. People do not like her daughter—spoiled, they say she is—and there was that ruckus with her brother. They all think the doctor is a love, even if they talk some about his lady friend, but that's really old news now. They do think it's only a matter of time before he trades his wife in for a newer model. I like Dale Reeves, and I know he has worked some miracles on some very desperate teeth. I think the ladies envy Roberta for her possession of him more than even her social clout, and that's why they're all hoping for a dramatic bust-up. You know, I pretend to understand you women, but I really don't. Sometimes I wonder if I wouldn't have been better off if I were gay, given my profession. My gay colleagues seem to get much better gossip than I do. It's not as if I'd share what I know with Amy . . ." Norman had an equally plump and jolly but fully tressed wife, and at least a couple of growing children.

"It's always something," Margaret said. "I'll see you in two weeks, usual time and day."

"Take care, darling." Norman bustled off to add a dash of hair spray to Audrey Cheever's coiffeur, and Margaret was left to think of what to do with herself for the rest of the day.

Chapter 8

What she did was stop by the rental offices of a few comparatively modest high-rise apartment buildings on her way home. A few had one-bedroom apartments available, although the rent seemed astronomical, even to Margaret, who paid the proverbial pretty penny for her own place.

She kept thinking of Lucy Rose as a typical unfunded young woman just starting out in New York, and she didn't believe that Roberta Reeves would be likely to pay her enough to afford a two-thousand-dollar-a-month apartment. Big Ed would have to kick in a substantial amount, or Carolyn Sue would have to come up with a low-rent, nice-neighborhood deal. Or maybe Lucy Rose had private wealth that would take care of vile necessities like rent. Come to think of it, though, hadn't Lucy and her nature-loving beau staged a fake kidnapping in order to acquire funds from Big Ed? That didn't seem to indicate that the girl was independently wealthy. Or maybe saving even a corner of the environment was far pricier than Margaret had imagined.

When she reached her own neighborhood, she remembered to stop at the locksmith shop on the corner and have an extra apartment key cut for Lucy. She didn't think she could handle too many two in the morning wake-up-and-let-me-in doorbells.

Margaret didn't know whether Lucy would return to the apartment for dinner, but as she sipped a chilled glass of white burgundy, she thought about sautéing some chicken breasts and melting some frozen vegetables in case her houseguest turned up hungry. Margaret certainly was, having merely drunk a latte and nibbled on a biscuit that Norman's staff had brought in for her. Dining out daily was too expensive to consider, and Lucy hadn't yet offered to pay her share of the food, although she certainly had enough money to tip the handyman and hop into a taxi on an impulse.

Lucy dragged in at six-thirty, looking far less like Ms. Young Businesswoman Sets Out to Conquer Manhattan than she had that morning.

"Have a glass of wine and tell me about the job," Margaret said. "Take off your shoes, change into jeans, get comfortable."

"I think I will," Lucy said. "It's not going to be easy until I get everything sorted out. Roberta's idea of organization is to throw something on a pile of papers and hope it gets done. Since she hates doing paperwork, it doesn't ever get done, and there are contracts for services to be signed, money to be collected and paid out, all sorts of things that simply must be done if she's going to pull off this reception and dinner dance for some disease that people are interested in. She hasn't even definitely booked the room yet. I kind of like him."

"You met Dale? I thought he worked late into the night, relieving the agonies of toothache among the rich and famous."

"Well, he showed around lunchtime. Roberta had already gone out to lunch with some friends while I toiled on, rearranging the piles and putting things into folders, so Dale took me out to eat. A fabulous Italian place. I stuffed myself, so don't worry about me needing anything tonight. He's so interesting and funny . . . and kind of sad, too. He told me that his birthday is in a couple of weeks, but he didn't think anybody would remember it, because they never have in the past. Not even his son or his daughter. We always have a big party for Big Ed's birthday, with barbecue and beans and cole slaw. Everybody comes. It's kind of like a national holiday."

Margaret, glad that she hadn't started dinner yet in spite of her increasing hunger, searched for memories of Dale Reeves, but none of them resonating were either interesting or funny.

"I always found Dale Reeves rather dull and doctorish," Margaret said. "I always had the feeling that he was inspecting me for possible ways to correct my overbite or the imperfection that proclaimed loudly that I am the typical victim of the British dental profession. What was he funny about?"

"He was kind of standoffish at first, I admit," Lucy said, "but then I got him talking about the time Roberta made him vacation at a dude ranch somewhere in Arizona, and he had to tell me about how poorly he related to horses, although he is deeply concerned about the great outdoors. I grew up with horses all around me, and of course, my mother met her end thanks to a horse, so we had plenty to talk about. I gather Roberta wasn't too happy about the riding life either, but I told him I'd show him the ropes when he visited me in Texas. I'll turn him into a cowboy so fast he won't recognize himself."

"I see," Margaret said. "And was Roberta pleased with your work?"

Lucy shrugged. "She hadn't come home by the time I left. Dale was in and out all afternoon, what there was left of it after lunch, but I came to a point where I didn't know what to do next, so I left her a note and came back here. Am I too bad for running out like that? I wanted to have time to shower and change clothes before I went out."

"Out?"

"Didn't I mention it? Frankie and some of the guys I met the other night made me promise to join them tonight at this new club that's just opened. Sounds like fun." Lucy left her nearly full wine glass and went off to prepare for another night on the town.

The phone rang while the shower was running. Margaret answered, hoping it was De Vere or Paul, or even Carolyn Sue with the promise of a home for Lucy. It was a deep male voice, but not one that Margaret recognized, and it wanted Lucy.

"She's not available at the moment," Margaret said cautiously. "Is there a message?"

"Tell her that Dale Reeves phoned," the voice said. Then added, "Is that you, Lady Margaret? I haven't seen you in ages. It's just that I half promised Lucy that I'd take her out to dinner tonight, but she was gone by the time I got back here. Roberta has some committee meeting or other tonight, and I hate to eat alone."

"I can't speak absolutely for Lucy," Margaret said, "but I understood that she had an engagement this evening." Things seemed to be moving fast even if Roberta hadn't planned to use Lucy as a diversion for Dale.

Dale made a sound that might have signified disappointment. "Just tell her I called. I'm going out of town tomorrow to see some colleagues in Boston. I'll catch up with her in a day or two."

"I'll do that," Margaret said. "My best to Roberta."

When Lucy reappeared in a robe, a towel around her wet hair, with her dark brows a slash of black, she looked like a mysterious Eastern princess. Remarkably attractive girl, Margaret thought, then said, "Dale Reeves called while you were in the shower."

Lucy seemed indifferent. "Wanting what?"

"He seemed to think he'd invited you out this evening, since Roberta has gone to a committee meeting."

"He didn't," she said. "And I think one meal a day with him is sufficient."

"I told him you were otherwise engaged."

"Good enough," Lucy said. "He's nice, but he's kind of old for me. He's going to be fifty."

"When a man's as attractive as Dale Reeves, fifty isn't so old."

Lucy's smile was unreadable. "He's got other women he can take out, I'm sure." She shrugged. "Men are like that. Of course, my mother is dead, so Daddy has a perfect right to see his lady friends, and he does." She shrugged again. "I barely know the man. That frump Roberta is lucky to have him, even if she does treat him like an old chair. She ought to be more attentive. Well, I'd better pull myself together and go on downtown, even though the guys say nothing much happens anywhere until late. Want to join us, Margaret? It sounds like fun."

It didn't sound like first-rate fun to Margaret. "I think I'll beg off tonight, unless you feel you need someone with you."

Lucy laughed. "Like protection? I don't think so, and I don't think I'll be late."

"Let me give you a key to the apartment," Margaret said. "In case you are late after all."

"I won't be. Roberta has a pile of stuff for me to do tomorrow. And I have to remind her that Dale's birthday is coming up, and we ought to celebrate it with something special. I want it to be a surprise party," Lucy said. "As soon as he told me about it today, I knew what I hope I can persuade Roberta to do. Or else I'll persuade his girlfriend."

"You seem to know a lot about Dale Reeves in a very short time."

"Apparently Roberta doesn't listen to him, and of course he can't talk about his girlfriend to her, so he talked to me. Her name's Lorna something, and I think she must be pretty old, probably Roberta's age, but I'll bet she's in better shape."

"Lorna Hutchison is a very attractive woman. I think she used to be a model, although nowadays she's the editor of an important fashion magazine," Margaret said.

"Huh, the models I met the other night didn't seem smart enough to read, let alone be the editor of something."

"I've met Lorna a few times, and found her quite intelligent, although I wasn't aware at the time that she was attached to Dale."

"You never do know, do you?" Lucy said. "I suppose I could get his son or his daughter to throw a party, but Dale said they aren't speaking to each other. Anyhow, I'd like to do it at the big apartment. You know, there's a terrace that almost wraps around the building. If we pray for nice weather, maybe we'll have an Indian Summer; that's what the kids in Massachusetts used to call warm fall days when I was at college. We could pull it off. Even if it was kind of cold, we could get heaters and stuff, and even a canopy in case of rain. Roberta has some little trees out on the terrace, and big cement pots with plants. They might be dead in a couple of weeks, but I could get chrysanthemums; they're good in the fall. A big birthday cake—it's his fiftieth birthday—and a ton of candles, sparklers even, little white lights all around and really good food. I'll bet I could round up some real Texas barbecue somewhere in New York, or I could make it myself if the snotty cook they have will let me into her kitchen. But it's a surprise, remember, so don't let on to anybody until I've made all the arrangements."

Margaret wondered who she could possibly tell that would make any difference. She certainly wouldn't be letting on to Dale. "My lips are sealed." Then she wondered why little Lucy Rose was making the arrangements and not Roberta. Well, as Lucy had mentioned, Roberta probably didn't remember it was her husband's birthday, and making arrangements was part of the reason Roberta had taken her on.

Half an hour later, Lucy was ready to have her way with New York nightlife. Wearing a glowing red outfit, with her dark hair shining from a wash, she would make a stunning appearance in the dim clubs downtown.

"Ah, Lucy, I wonder if it's wise to wear all that jewelry out at night. It could attract unwelcome attention from needy muggers." Margaret looked anxiously at what Lucy was wearing in the way of bijoux.

Lucy looked surprised. "I wear this stuff all the time at home." The "stuff" was a flashing diamond brooch and stud earrings, a couple of large rings, which, if not diamonds, were certainly eye-catching.

"That's the point," Margaret said. "This isn't home; it's big, bad New York." She felt like an overly cautious old auntie just saying it.

"I'll be okay," Lucy said. "Anyhow, I've hired a limo to drive me to the club, wait around for me, and bring me back. I don't want Frankie getting the idea that I hang around with him just for the sake of a ride home. Besides, the people I'm meeting aren't needy muggers. See you in the morning."

Well, she's settling in, Margaret thought. At least her room is so small she won't be tempted to bring someone home for the night.

Indeed, if little Lucy had the foresight to hire a limo to chauffeur her about New York, she would surely have the foresight to book a hotel room if she planned a romantic tryst with an environmentally sound young man met at Moomba or Limelight.

Yet, was all of this proper behavior? Would Carolyn Sue approve of Margaret allowing Lucy to behave in such a manner—nightclubbing almost every night, driving about in a hired limo, lunching with the attractive Dale Reeves, planning his birthday party? And who knew what else little Lucy had been up to?

Wait a minute. Margaret's job description definitely did not include supervising the morals and social activities of this Texas lass. All Margaret had to do, really, was make sure Lucy stayed alive. Nothing more.

Chapter 9

Having paid a substantial amount to have Norman design her hair, Margaret felt she really ought to take the opportunity to show herself off to somebody. De Vere likely wouldn't notice, but Paul might. He'd spent enough years observing his mother deck her person out in new clothes, jewels, and hairstyles with the expectation that he would comment approvingly. He would surely notice Margaret and remark on how attractive she looked. Maybe it was an Italian male thing.

"What are you up to tonight?" she asked when Paul answered the phone.

"I am unfortunately gravely lacking in funds, so I intend to watch terrifically bad movies on television." He sounded forlorn.

"Care to escort me someplace this evening?"

"Where?"

"Anywhere you choose. My treat."

"I'm not sure the places I'd choose would be to your liking," Paul said. "There are some new clubs downtown, but . . ."

"I have a 'but' also. But I'm afraid we'd run into Lucia Rose. She just went out to meet some fellows she met the other night when she went out to the clubs. What was your 'but'?"

"But I think they would not be to your taste, with or without the presence of Lucy. I told you to be afraid."

"Paul, she's perfectly nice, just a bit overwhelmed by the excitement of New York. Of course, she does seem highly skilled at attracting young men."

"Not to change the subject, but have you had dinner?"

The chicken breasts were still wrapped up cosily in the refrigerator. She could cook them another day. "No, and I'm very hungry," she said.

"We'll go to Campagna. You like Mark's cooking. I'll fix up a reservation, and meet you there in an hour. Can you handle that?"

"Done," Margaret said, and in just a minute or two over an hour later, she was sipping a Campari soda in Campagna's pleasant, semirustic surroundings and listening to Paul instruct the waiter to bring them whatever the chef recommended that evening.

"I need a favor," Margaret said. "Not social, nothing critical."

Paul raised an eyebrow and waited.

"I may need you to put some pressure on your mother to help me find Lucy Rose an apartment of her own. She's no trouble, really, but I shall go bonkers if she ends up living with me indefinitely. There's not enough room, I feel I have to be looking out for her all the time, and I don't want to get mixed up in any tangled relationships she may find herself in with Roberta and Dale Reeves. Carolyn Sue rather half promised she'd look into the matter, but I'm afraid she'll get caught up in her travels or reconstructing her house or something, and the Lucy question will slip her mind. Will you help?"

"I can certainly call my mother and berate her for putting you in this situation. She herself is very sensitive about having all the space she wants, so she'll understand your plight. I can even put some pressure on old Ben, who's a great pal of Big Ed's. Ben will do favors for me as long as it doesn't cost him or my mother any money. I think," Paul added gloomily, "that Ben is thinking of running for public office. He'll need Big Ed's help if he does."

"Then that's settled," Margaret said. "It will certainly take a burden off of my shoulders. But I must still keep track of Lucy. She tends to fly off in all directions, not always thinking first about consequences."

The food was delicious, and they drank some excellent wine, also recommended by the staff. The bill when it came was hefty, but Margaret paid gladly and was proud of herself for not pumping Paul about De Vere's recent activities, until they found themselves outside.

"Have you been enjoying the fish that Sam brought back from Connecticut?" she asked.

"I do not care for bluefish," Paul said. "At least not the way I could manage to prepare it. De Vere does not cook, as you well know. His father stayed the night with us before returning to New Jersey. He's a fine gentleman. I might have been better off if my own father were more like him."

So now she knew that De Vere had actually been somewhere that produced bluefish. She mentally kicked herself for being suspicious. It was really none of her business where Sam De Vere went, and with whom.

Paul said, "The club I was thinking of visiting is only a block or two away. Shall we walk?"

"Of course. Suddenly I feel like being somewhere where there's music and dancing and beautiful people."

There were all of those things at Iris, which had opened only a month before to great press fanfare. Margaret even remembered a story in *The Daily News* or *The New York Post* about an unseemly brawl that had broken out at the inaugural party and had caused Robert De Niro to flee the premises. Someone had managed to photograph him looking distressed about being caught in such a situation.

The doorkeeper/bouncer was a burly youth who apparently spent his nonworking hours in a gym, building up his pecs and abs and practicing his scowl to keep at bay the Bridge and Tunnel crowd, the youthful clubland wanna-bes who ventured over and under the river into Manhattan from Brooklyn and Queens and New Jersey.

He greeted Paul warmly and then, to Margaret's surprise, bowed to her and said, "Long time no see, Lady Margaret. You're looking real fine tonight."

Margaret blinked. First of all, someone, even someone as unlikely as this person, appeared to appreciate Norman's efforts on behalf of her hair. But how did he know her?

"I'm sorry, I don't . . ."

"Sure, you wouldn't remember me. I do some work for Eddie Leone, remember? He used to drive for Mr. Anton, and he was always talking about you. Back when all those airy-fairy decorators were working on the house Anton owned in the Eighties."

"Ah, yes," Margaret said. "How is Eddie? I haven't seen him for a long time." Eddie had been ninety percent thug but a one hundred percent devoted employee of Peter Anton and—small world—Richard Centner,

Roberta's one-time romance. Eddie had developed a mild crush on Margaret during Gloria Anton's ill-fated designer show house. She winced at the thought that this chance meeting with one of his buddies would inspire Eddie to rekindle his passion.

"Eddie's doing fine," the bouncer said. "Last I heard he was out in Vegas handling stuff for one of the casinos. I coulda gone with him, but I don't like that heat. Besides, I'm New York through and through. Hey!" He paused to lay a large hand on the chest of a preppy-looking youth who was trying to make an end run around the velvet rope and into the club. "Back in line, buddy, until I say you go in. You two go right on in, though."

He waved Margaret and Paul toward the door, and the two of them entered a huge, cavernous space. Margaret thought she heard a few hisses behind her back, signifying the displeasure of the patient crowd that didn't rate admittance. But the hisses were soon drowned out by the amplified sound of the DJ's records, and the constant low mutter of the crowd inside. Lights flashed on and off, and now and then Margaret saw illuminated, handsome faces on the dance floor, some of whom she almost recognized.

And the face she did recognize belonged, of course, to little Lucy, perched on a stool at the end of the bar, surrounded by a clutch of young men who pressed in on her as if to claim a piece of her. She was laughing, and with her dark good looks, her face almost disappeared into the darker background.

Then she spotted Margaret and waved her over.

"Margaret, and Paul, too. You said you didn't want to come out with me, and here you are. Meet Frankie and

Bob and . . . what's your name again, honey?" The blond boy she had spoken to tossed his mane of hair and withdrew from the group. "He's sort of shy," Lucy said. "Not my type, really. Move over, Frankie. Give Lady Margaret a bar stool. Margaret, this is Frankie Martinez. And Paul, sweetie, it's been ages since I've seen you. Your mother said you were getting married. Not to Margaret, I assume."

"No," Paul said, "but a man couldn't find a finer woman. You'll have to come around and meet Georgina the next time she's in New York. She's home in England for a few weeks just now."

"I expect to be in New York for as long as I live," Lucy said, "so I'm looking forward to meeting her."

Just then, Frankie, who hadn't done more than nod briefly when introduced, grabbed Lucy by the arm, and they went off to join the throbbing masses on the dance floor.

"I'll have another Campari soda," Margaret said, "but I really don't care to spend hours here. It's a bit too frenetic for my taste."

"Half an hour, then," Paul said. "I want to roam around a bit and see who's here." He slipped away into the very handsome crowd, only here and there interrupted by some outlandishly dressed boy or girl. It was hard to define their sex, although the heavy makeup might be a clue. Their costumes didn't give a hint. Club kids. The bouncer didn't seem to have let too many of the extreme getups in, but there were enough to give the place a bit of bizarre color. Margaret noticed a couple of rather large drag queens holding court at a corner table. The black one with the blond wig was quite stunning— could it be RuPaul?—although his/her companion seemed to have a slight five-o'clock shadow and a rather scary red wig.

Margaret sipped her drink thoughtfully, if thought was possible under the particular acoustic circumstances. She fended off half a dozen sudden admirers, and kept an eye on Lucy, who was gyrating and spinning around the dance floor with abandon, still under the control of Frankie. Still, it looked harmless enough, and Lucy seemed absolutely delighted. In a few moments, she returned to the bar and said, "If you want to borrow my limo to take you home, please do. I'm going to be here for a while, so just send the car back when you're finished with it. It's the long white number just outside. The driver is called Shakir. He's okay. Tell him I sent you."

As soon as Margaret caught Paul's eye, she signaled him to join her. When he had disengaged himself from the clutches of a very pretty but remarkably emaciated wench—one of those anorexic models, perhaps—she told him she was borrowing Lucy's limo to take her home, and it would be back shortly. "She'll probably give you a lift home, unless you want to leave with me now."

"I think I should stay with her," Paul said seriously. "That Frankie Martinez she's hooked up with isn't a truly upstanding citizen. In fact, he's been called a drug merchant, catering to the customers of the clubs that will allow him in. I heard he just barely escaped arrest only a couple of days ago. The people he associates with are even more unsavory, if you ask me, and you could also ask De Vere. It's the least I can do for my mother's old friend's daughter. Keep watch in case things get rough. The mayor has it in for the clubs that are allowing open drug dealing. And don't worry. I don't do drugs myself, and if Lucy so much as hints at it, I'll personally put her on a plane back to Texas."

"You're too good," Margaret said. "The car should be back in half an hour or less. Suggest that Lucy go home then, or at least make some new friends. Maybe there's a calmer venue where she can enjoy the nightlife. She'll probably listen to you since you've known her for far longer than I have."

"Little Lucy knows her own mind," Paul said. "I've known that forever. I'll see if she'll go somewhere else with me. The club guys all know me, so I can usually get in anywhere. Besides, I'm presentable."

That you are, Margaret thought. Tall, dark-haired, and truly handsome. If your father looked anything like you when Carolyn Sue met him, it's no wonder she snapped him up matrimonially.

"Ah . . . you didn't say where De Vere was tonight," Margaret said, unable to keep herself from asking. She hated herself for doing so.

"He said he was going to be working late, since he's been away for a few days and has to catch up. I think he has to be in court tomorrow for some case he's been working on. Margaret," he said seriously, "honestly, to the best of my knowledge, he is not out with another woman."

"I didn't ask that," she said, and knew she sounded angry. "Sorry, I didn't mean to be sharp with you. I was just wondering."

Margaret fled Iris and its noisy babble and throbbing music, and found Shakir half a block away, dozing in the driver's seat of a battleship-sized white limo. He sped her home, with the promise to return to the club to fetch Lucy and Paul with no delays.

Margaret faintly heard Lucy return to the apartment either very late that evening or very early the next morning, depending on one's point of view. She listened briefly, and determined that Lucy had not invited anyone in for a nightcap or something more tasty.

I'll have to have a talk with that girl, Margaret thought as she sank again into deep slumber. Her dreams were shot through with the flashing lights of Iris, and she imagined that she and De Vere had taken to the crowded dance floor to gyrate the night away, and then suddenly he was gone, and she saw him gliding past with Lucy Rose in his arms. In the morning, when she remembered her dream, she was puzzled. De Vere was not a dancer, and she didn't for a moment believe that Lucy Rose was the type of young thing he'd take to.

After a brief moment of insecurity, tinged with jealousy that Lucy Rose would dare to show up in her dream, she got up and went to see whether her roommate was prepared for another day under the eyes of Roberta Reeves. All too often, she'd discovered, these young things had the impression that work was something they did when they chose to, rather than an obligation that they had to meet, whether or not they felt like it.

Lucy was up and dressed and drinking coffee when Margaret made her way to the kitchen. She wore yet another perfectly coordinated outfit, today a charcoal gray pantsuit with a red silk blouse and red shoes. A red handbag that looked like Prada was on the kitchen table.

"Now, wasn't last night fun?" Lucy said. She looked very chipper, in spite of the late hour of her return.

"Fun enough for those who can handle that sort of thing. It wears me out rather quickly. Did Paul get driven home?"

"Oh, sure. It wasn't far. You know, Paul's a lot more fun than I remembered, and he's turned out to be very good-looking. More than he was when I knew him back in Dallas. And I've booked Shakir for tonight, too. It's so much more convenient than finding a taxi, don't you think?"

"I think," Margaret said carefully, "that you and I ought to have a talk tonight before you go out."

"Of course," Lucy said, "unless . . ." She didn't finish her sentence, merely grabbed her handbag and headed for the door. "I should be back around the same time as yesterday, unless something unexpected turns up that I have to deal with." She had a smug sort of smile that made Margaret wonder what she was going to contrive to have turn up unexpectedly. Dale Reeves at loose ends, perhaps?

Stop it, Margaret told herself. You don't know that little Lucy is planning anything, especially with regard to Dale, and given Roberta's hit-or-miss way of conducting her affairs, no doubt something unexpected would turn up. And if it did, Margaret would arrange her little talk with Lucy for another day.

"See you later," Lucy said. "You know, I never thought I'd actually look forward to going to a job. With my father's events, when I got bored with them, I used to just shut my door and go back to sleep, and let the help order the food and arrange the flowers. I feel a positive need to straighten out things at the Reeves' place. This is much more fun, because I know I'm going to make a difference. I can't thank you enough for finding the job for me, Margaret."

"You're welcome," Margaret said. "I'm glad everything is working out for you."

Lucy paused at the kitchen door. "It would really, really work out better if I had more closet space for my clothes." She shrugged. "Well, you can't be blamed for the size of your apartment."

Then she was gone. Margaret wondered briefly if she would be blamed for committing a symbolic murder in this situation. Perhaps simply for grabbing armloads of Lucy's frocks from the closet and stuffing them down the trash chute in the hall. She took a deep breath and hurried to find her address book, where she was certain she'd written down Carolyn Sue's mobile phone number.

Chapter 10

"*Don't you worry* your pretty head," Carolyn Sue said. "I've got it all taken care of. This fellow, Richie, who handles my real estate affairs, is goin' to be callin' you in the next couple days, and he's got some places lined up that would be okay for Lucy. Is she behavin' herself?"

Margaret didn't know what to say. Lucy hadn't actually misbehaved, but she was becoming a trial. Margaret couldn't get away from the feeling that she bore the responsibility for the girl's safety in the city.

"At least she seems to be getting along well with Roberta Reeves."

"What's she got to do with that creature? I don't know why she has a hair on her head the way she abuses it."

"She speaks well of you," Margaret said. "Lucy is acting as her personal assistant, for the present. I must have told you that I had something lined up." But she knew she hadn't said anything specific to Carolyn Sue.

"Just so long as she keeps out of reach of that tooth wrangler Roberta is married to."

"Dale is apparently quite taken with Lucy Rose," Margaret said cautiously. "They've lunched, and Lucy is planning his birthday party."

"You keep an eye on that girl. I don't want her takin' up with unsuitable men."

"She seems quite able to take care of herself," Margaret said. "She's gone out to the clubs two nights she's been here. I believe she's met some nice young men." Not counting Frankie, the alleged drug dealer. "Paul joined us last evening."

"Well, that's just fine. I hope the young men are from good families."

"Possibly," Margaret said. "Families of some sort, in any event."

"I once fancied Lucy as a perfect match for Paul, but they didn't hit it off, more's the pity. Now, if Richie doesn't take care of things about the apartment, you let me know and I'll take care of him." Then she asked casually, "How's that dear boy Sam treatin' you?"

"Sam treats me well," Margaret said. She didn't care to get into a discussion of her rather pallid romantic life just now. "He's promised me some fish."

"No kind of gift to give a sweetheart. The boy needs a talkin'-to." Her disapproving tone indicated that De Vere would get a severe talking-to when Carolyn Sue next descended upon Manhattan.

Actually, Margaret thought the promise of bluefish was rather touching. "He and his father went fishing for a few days. He's just bringing home the kill, like a proper hunting male."

"And you hang around the East Side gatherin' while he's huntin'." She sighed. "As long as I can rest easy about little Lucy, I suppose I shouldn't take on any worry about you. I do appreciate what you're doing for the child."

Margaret gritted her teeth and said, "It's a pleasure having her here, Carolyn Sue. Anything for a friend."

Sure enough, before the day was over, someone called and identified himself as calling per instructions from Carolyn Sue. "Are you the Lady Margaret Priam who was running that show house some time ago?"

"The very same," she said. As if there were a parade of Lady Margaret Priams along the avenues of Manhattan. She was also puzzled that he knew about her and the show house.

"I guess we could consider ourselves old friends. This is Richard Centner. We met when I was working with Peter Anton."

"So we did," Margaret said, and flashed back to the unpleasantness of that event, and Richard Centner's peripheral involvement in somewhat shady real estate dealings. "Are you actually working for Carolyn Sue?" First Eddie Leone and now Centner had bubbled to the surface of her life.

"After his wife died, Anton's real estate business kind of went south, and I didn't have a partner anymore. We sold off the house where you held the show house, did pretty well, but in the end we both lost quite a bit of money. I got to know Carolyn Sue through a mutual friend also in real estate, and I found out she needed someone to oversee her residential holdings in New York, and you know Carolyn Sue . . . 'Richie, honey, do you think you could help out a kinda helpless woman and take charge of things for me?' I certainly know the real estate business, and she's generous with her remuneration, so I took on the job. What's your problem that Carolyn Sue wants me to help with?"

Margaret said, "It's really minor. A young woman who's a friend of Carolyn Sue's has moved here from Dallas, and has been staying with me. I don't have enough room for two people, so I asked Carolyn Sue if there were any suitable apartments in one of her buildings for the girl."

It had seemed so easy to ask Carolyn Sue, but now Margaret realized she was talking to the man that gossip said had been involved with Roberta Reeves, Lucy's employer. "Maybe I should just look around myself, and not trouble you."

Surely Carolyn Sue followed New York gossip closely, and as soon as Margaret mentioned Roberta, she would have recalled the rumors about Richard and Roberta.

Just to test the situation, or to make it more complicated, Margaret said, "Lucy is working for Roberta Reeves as a sort of social secretary. I was kind of hoping that Roberta had a spare room in her big apartment for Lucy, but . . ." Certainly Centner would know whether Roberta had extra space.

"I happen to know Roberta Reeves," Centner said. "Used to squire her about a bit in days past, don't see much of her anymore. I do know the Reeves apartment, though, and I can't recall a single empty room. She has quarters for the maid, but she wouldn't dream of giving up her live-in servant. Her daughter, Susan, and the son keep rooms there in case they have a tiff with their spouses and want to go home to Mummy and Daddy. Roberta would never surrender the couple of small guest rooms she has because she loves to invite people to stay for the weekend. No, unless Susan or the son can be persuaded to give up their space, I don't think there's any hope for your girl there."

"It was just a hope," Margaret said. "How about an apartment in a Carolyn Sue building? Lucy's father is reportedly rich, so she could pay the going rate. I think she'd like to be near to Roberta, since she's taking her job very seriously, and wants to be available at a moment's notice."

"Carolyn Sue's best places are in Chelsea, not very close to mid–Park Avenue. She's invested in some buildings in Harlem because she thinks it's going to be big in a couple of years, but I wouldn't suggest One Hundred and Twenty-fifth Street for an innocent from out of town."

Centner paused, and Margaret hoped he was thinking hard. "Wait a minute," he said. "Carolyn Sue bought a couple of buildings between Lexington and Third, in the Sixties. They're still mostly occupied, but she's thinking of working a deal with the city to tear them down and build a nice, modern medium-high high-rise. The neighborhood association isn't friendly to the idea, but some of the tenants are getting nervous and have been talking about moving out. Could be that there will be a few empty apartments for the short-term, until Carolyn Sue gets the variances and so forth to start construction. Want me to look into it?"

"Definitely," Margaret said. Then she thought that maybe Lucy could live in one of the suites at the Villa d'Este, Carolyn Sue's little luxury midtown hotel. Several people she knew, including the late Gloria Anton, had maintained pieds-à-terre there. It was expensive, but there were always Big Ed's deep pockets to fall back on.

"I'll think about the possibilities," Centner said, "and give you a call in a couple of days. We'll figure something out. Carolyn Sue has spoken."

Margaret felt a bit of relief after Centner's call. She wanted to believe that matters would be resolved promptly, especially after she ventured into her bedroom and discovered that Lucy had stored two heavy suitcases at the foot of her bed. She supposed that she could check with her building's rental office to see if there was a larger apartment available, except that she knew she couldn't afford the higher rent it would surely carry.

While everyone was wrestling with Lucy Rose's housing problem, Lucy herself was in the throes of reorganizing everything in Roberta's cluttered drawing room/office. She'd gotten as far as separating the documents for the three major charity events into three piles. Now she was going through the piles one by one and putting the papers in some kind of order, making a checklist of things already done, that needed to be done, or that hadn't yet even been thought of.

As midday approached, she kept glancing at her watch and at the door. Roberta, she knew, was again out lunching with friends, but had promised to bring a few of them back after lunch to meet Lucy. "They're on my committees," she'd told Lucy, "and I do want you to know them, because you'll be working closely with them."

Just what I need, she thought as she glanced at a proof of an invitation for a benefit to aid the homeless. The invitations had to be printed, addressed, and mailed in the next week if the event was to have a respectable attendance, but apparently Roberta hadn't even checked the proof, which contained at least three spelling errors, much less instructed the printer to start printing it. And she herself would have to double-check the spelling of the names of all the committee members and patrons listed on the invitation. She put that task at the top of her list, and stood up. It was exactly noon.

She slipped quietly out of the drawing room into the darkened foyer. No sight or sound of the maid or the cook. Well, the cook had said she was going out to do some shopping because the Reeves were having guests for dinner, and since the maid had almost nothing to do but answer the door and hang up Roberta's clothes, she was probably lying down in her room, watching television. There was no one about to wonder why Lucy was roaming around the apartment. If anyone did ask, she'd say she was going to the powder room, which was way down at the end of the hall. As she walked along the hallway, she stopped at each door, opened it, and peered in. The largest room was the master bedroom, and then came two dreadfully small guest rooms. Finally, she found what she thought must be Susan's room, separated from her brother Greg's room by a large bathroom.

She looked at her watch. It was about the time that Dale Reeves had shown up the day before and taken her to lunch, but there was no sign of him today. She wasn't interested in food, but she had enjoyed being ushered in to that divine restaurant, with the maître d' hovering and the waiters dying to fill their water glasses and take their order. People did seem eager to make way for the well-known Dr. Reeves, or to stop at his table to chat. He had introduced her as "my wife's young friend from Texas," which was all right, but she would have preferred to be just his young friend. One woman, a Mrs. Cheever, according to Dale, had eyed her closely, and had gushed, "I've heard so much about you!" Impossible, since she'd only been in town a couple of days, and she didn't think that Mrs. Cheever frequented any of the clubs Lucy had visited.

These society women were worse than the ones she knew in Dallas, only she didn't believe that Texas ladies made up stories on the spot, at least not without a very good reason.

Lucy made her way into the big formal living room and walked to the far wall, where heavy drapes covered glass doors leading out to the wraparound terrace. She removed the bar that kept the doors firmly locked against intruders. How in the world would anyone be able to reach the seventeenth floor from a busy street and attempt to gain entrance? There must be easier places to rob in New York, but then, she'd heard that New York burglars weren't especially bright.

She stepped out onto the terrace, where an array of comfortable chaises upholstered in white-and-dark-blue canvas were lined up along the parapet. She looked over the edge, and grew dizzy at the sight of the street so many stories below. This side of the building faced a side street, not Park Avenue, so she could see some scraggly New York trees lining the street, and a deep-maroon canopy over a side entrance to the apartment building.

The plants in their cement pots looked a bit weary after a long, hot summer, and there were a few brave trees in planters scattered about the terrace. She could imagine what the birthday party would look like. A long table there, loaded with food, a bar beside the doors, lots of chairs and little tables, and the whole place strung with colored lights. She'd decided that white lights were common. Maybe she'd have all blue with just a few white ones here and there, or strings of multicolored lights. She could almost smell the barbecue, and the big pot of beans. She could even almost hear the sound of country western music playing low in the background. And then, the big moment, a giant cake—maybe several layers, like a wedding cake, but covered with candles—being wheeled out, and everybody singing "Happy Birthday."

All she had to do was convince Roberta to do it. If she could persuade Roberta that she didn't have to do a thing, she'd certainly agree. She'd make sure that Roberta invited Margaret, and even Paul. She didn't think Frankie would fit in, though.

It was going to be a killer evening.

Chapter 11

"*A*nybody home?" Lucy whirled around at the sound of the woman's voice coming from inside the apartment. She left the terrace and carefully slipped back inside and looked around. "Mother? Mrs. Frost? Carlotta? Damn, where is everybody?"

Lucy edged carefully through the big room, to the hall, and peered out. A young woman in her twenties wearing a fussy print dress and too much makeup was standing in the hall with her hands on her hips. She had been calling for her mother, so this must be Roberta's daughter, Susan, who was going to guide Lucy through the pitfalls of New York society. Not a chance.

Lucy stepped into the hallway.

"Who the hell are you?" Susan asked conversationally.

"Lucia Rose Grant. I'm your mother's new assistant. She's lunching out with friends, and Mrs. Frost is shopping. I don't know where Carlotta is."

"Well, I'm Susan Dillon, if you're interested. What are you doing prying into my mother's private things?"

"I'm not prying." Lucy didn't bother to disguise her indignance. "I've been working on Roberta's charity files since early this morning, and I was just stretching my legs out on the terrace, getting some fresh air. Roberta told me I was free to go anyplace I liked in the apartment. She should be back in an hour or so, and Mrs. Frost will also be back soon. I'm sure you know your way around, if you want to get a cold drink or something." Lucy was determined she was not going to fetch and carry for this rude person.

"I don't want anything. I just dropped by to see my mother. She's always complaining that I never come around, and when I do get a chance to stop by, she's never here. Sometimes I like to spend the weekend here when I get bored with my husband and our place up in Westchester. Mother keeps a room just for me." As if a room was some kind of reward for good behavior, something Susan apparently didn't have a taste for, along with manners.

"I'm sure you can take care of yourself," Lucy said. "I have to get back to work."

Back in Roberta's lair, Lucy busied herself with her many tasks, but half her mind was on the idea of Susan's seldom-used room, which was certainly a lot bigger than that closet Margaret called a guest room. At the same time, she kept an ear cocked for the possible arrival of Dale. His office wasn't far away, and he'd told her he often liked to return home during his lunch break.

Then the phone rang on Roberta's desk. She'd told Lucy to answer that line, a private one, but not the others in the house, which were handled by the maid or Mrs. Frost or an answering machine.

"Hello?"

"Lucy, is that you?"

"Hello, Dale. I was just thinking of you."

"Is my wife out?"

"Yes. With some committee ladies, and then she said

something about a fitting, but your daughter is here somewhere."

"Her. Well, I was going to try to get away about now and see you, but something came up. And since Susan is around . . . never mind. Are you free for dinner tonight?"

"I suppose I could be," Lucy said, and grinned in spite of herself. She could give the clubs a rest for one night.

"I'll pick you up at Lady Margaret's place around eight. Okay? Just give me her address." He was silent for a second. "Ah, Lucy, I assume that Lady Margaret is . . . discreet, but she does know Roberta, and all, and I wouldn't want her telling tales that might get blown all out of proportion. So maybe it would be better for you to meet me downstairs in front of her building."

"Margaret wouldn't say anything, I'm sure," Lucy said, being sure only that Margaret would have something to say to her, "but you're right. I'll be downstairs at eight, and then there won't be any problem at all."

After the call, Lucy wondered why Dale wasn't escorting his lady friend, Lorna, to dinner rather than her. It didn't matter, really. And even if Lorna had been a model once, she couldn't be so young now, and Lucy was.

"Do you have my mother's permission to take personal calls on her phone?" Susan was standing in the doorway, looking remarkably sour.

"It was a business call," Lucy said smoothly. "And yes, she did instruct me to answer this phone. We have all kinds of people calling, about tickets to events, the printers, the committee ladies . . . someone has to answer them, and that's my job when Roberta isn't here."

"I can't waste any more time waiting for Mother. Tell her I was here." Susan looked Lucy up and down. "You know, you're quite a good-looking girl. I hope you manage to keep out of trouble in New York."

"I'm quite able to take care of myself," Lucy said, loathing Susan Dillon with a depth of feeling she'd seldom experienced. No way was this bitch going to show her any kind of ropes at all, not if Lucia Rose Grant had any say in the matter.

"Be seeing you," Susan said, and departed, brushing rudely past the cook, Mrs. Frost, who had just returned from shopping, but was carrying only a little shopping bag with the name of a well-known pastry shop on it.

"And good day to you, too, miss," Mrs. Frost muttered, as Susan made her way to the elevators. "And what did Madame's little treasure want?" she asked Lucy.

Lucy shrugged. "She said she just came to see her mother."

"Probably checking to be sure Madame hasn't sold off the Georgian silver tea set she expects to inherit, if she doesn't steal it first." Mrs. Frost was a sensible and stout woman who had treated Lucy kindly so far.

"Mrs. Frost," Lucy said, "I need to ask your advice. What if Mrs. Reeves were to give Dr. Reeves a surprise birthday party in about a week? On that Saturday? We could have it on the terrace, and I'd cook some things we like in Texas. You wouldn't have to do a thing except show me where things are kept. I'd be really careful in your kitchen. And I'd clean up afterward. I used to do that sort of thing all the time when my father had a party. He didn't like catered food, so I learned to cook really well. Not as good as you, of course," she added hastily. "Carlotta could help pass around the food, and maybe we could hire a bartender for the drinks, and even waiters to help Carlotta. I'd order the cake from that pastry shop." She indicated the bag Mrs. Frost was carrying. "Or any place else you think would be better. You would know much more about things like that than I do."

"Now, that's a nice idea, dear," Mrs. Frost said. "Poor Dr. Reeves doesn't get much attention from the family. Even his boy, Gregory, doesn't have much to do with his father. Of course, you'd have to get Madame's approval, but I'm willing to do what I can. The doctor has been very good to me and Carlotta over the years. Nice money gifts at Christmas, and he never forgets our birthdays. Probably because everybody forgets his."

"I'll speak to Mrs. Reeves as soon as she gets home," Lucy said. "I'll bet she says yes, as long as I keep up with the charity events she's organizing."

"We've got six extra people for dinner tonight. I'd better get to work," Mrs. Frost said wearily. "Madame always wants something special when the doctor is entertaining his professional friends."

Lucy stared unhappily at Mrs. Frost's back as she left for the kitchen. How would it be possible to dine with Dale if he was entertaining colleagues here for dinner tonight? She was almost surprised at the disappointment she was feeling. Then she took a deep breath and sat up straight at the desk. Dale was a perfectly nice older man, very good-looking, to be sure, an important man with a lot of obligations, plus a wife. Still, he did seem interested in her—the way most men tended to find her, well, she had to admit it, somewhat irresistible.

She could live with the disappointment, but she would certainly be waiting for him at the appointed time, just to see what happened. And when he failed to show, she'd have a bit more leverage over him. And she'd use it.

Lucy spent the afternoon happily arranging Dale Reeves' birthday party, only occasionally devoting some energy to Roberta's affairs. But she felt she'd made so much progress in just two days that she could afford to attend to other, more important matters for a couple of hours.

When Roberta finally returned home, late in the afternoon, she was in almost as vile a temper as her daughter had been. She snapped at Lucy when Lucy reminded her that the printer's proof of the invitation was overdue and had to be okayed to get the printing done in time. "Don't I have enough to do without these damned details?"

"I've checked all the names against the master list," Lucy said meekly, "and corrected some typos. So if you could just give it a quick look, I'll take care of it from there. I've spoken to Mrs. Thompson about the program for the dinner, and she's faxing a list of the ads that have been taken. She says you're doing very well with ad pages, and you'll be able to cover any costs that haven't been underwritten and still make a profit. Today I couldn't reach the lady in charge of ticket sales for the hospital benefit, but as of yesterday, it was about sixty percent sold out."

"Call Poppy Dill and tell her I need an item about the hospital thing in 'Social Scene,' as soon as possible. With the phone number to call for tickets. Give her a list of the big-name attendees. Meryl Streep has promised to come, and one of those huge basketball players from the Knicks. What's his name?"

"Patrick Ewing?" As it happened, Big Ed was a devotee of the NBA, so Lucy had spent many a tedious hour watching the Dallas Mavericks basketball team lope up and down the court. Of course she knew about Patrick

Ewing. The Knicks were a big draw when they came to town, and her Boston college friends always remembered that he was a hometown hero.

"That's the one, Ewing. Very tall. And you mention anybody else to her worth mentioning. Her number's in my Rolodex. Look at the time! I hope Mrs. Frost is getting dinner under way. Dale and I are expecting guests in just four hours."

Lucy said bravely, "It would probably be a good idea for you to remind Dr. Reeves about your dinner party. You never know when a man is going to get so involved with his work that he completely forgets engagements. My father couldn't ever remember what day he had promised to do anything."

Roberta softened. "You're right, dear. Why don't you call Dale and remind him?"

"I think it would be better coming from you," Lucy said. "It would sound forward coming from me." She wasn't going to let Dale off the hook by being the one to remind him he'd made two engagements for the same night, and one of them was with her.

"All right. You get on to Poppy, while I call Dale and get ready for this evening. I'll see you tomorrow at the usual time."

Lucy dutifully called Poppy Dill, although she had only the vaguest idea who the woman was. Some sort of columnist, she gathered. Margaret must have mentioned her.

"Miss Dill? This is Lucy Grant. I work for Roberta Reeves, and she asked me to call about the Dodge Memorial Hospital Benefit. It's in two weeks, and we're hoping to raise . . ."

"I know about it," Poppy said shortly. "You can tell

Roberta I'm running a short item at the end of the week."

"Thank you so much. Roberta wanted me to remind you that Patrick Ewing has accepted, and . . . and I could fax you the whole list of expected guests, in case you want to mention more of them."

"Thank you, dear, but you mailed me a list earlier this week."

"An updated list, then. It would help attract the public, and it's for such a good cause."

Poppy allowed Lucy to go through her spiel, and then said, "You must be Carolyn Sue's young friend that Lady Margaret mentioned."

"Yes." She was puzzled. Why would Margaret mention her to an unknown society columnist in New York?

"I intend to mention in my column that you're establishing yourself here in New York, to give you a sort of position to work from."

"I didn't know I needed such a thing," Lucy said. "Is it necessary?"

"Indeed it is. It's very useful," Poppy said. "The nice people will want to meet you. They'll invite you to parties and such, and introduce you to the best people in society."

"I am already meeting the best people just by working for Roberta."

"Hmm. There's good and then there's the best."

Lucy frowned. Was she saying that Roberta wasn't considered the best?

"You can tell your boss that you talked me into writing up her benefit. That should do you some good with her."

"Thank you, Miss Dill. I'm sure Roberta would be

glad to send you complimentary tickets so you could attend the benefit."

"I think not," Poppy said, and Lucy thought she heard something like horror in Poppy Dill's voice.

She puzzled over that as she put away her papers, turned out the lights, and headed back to Margaret's apartment.

Chapter 12

Margaret was out when Lucy got in, and she rather enjoyed having the apartment to herself so she could think in peace about the date with Dale that probably wouldn't happen. She wondered whether, after Roberta called to remind him of their dinner party, he would try to call her to cancel the evening's plans, or would he find a way to get out of the dinner party altogether?

You're being a fool, she told herself. You have no rights where Dale Reeves is concerned. She really did hate the idea of sneaking around behind his wife's back. She'd much prefer to be the hostess of the dinner party, efficiently running all those committees herself, and being praised by the beneficiaries of the charities that raised millions of dollars to make their lives easier, healthier, happier.

She went to the awful little room she called her own, and frowned. She'd looked around the Reeves' apartment when no one was around, and had seen the huge bedroom/sitting room that probably belonged to Susan. But neither that room nor Dale's son's room contained any sentimental reminders of their childhood, like teddy bears and picture books, although Gregory Reeves' room did have a Dartmouth banner on the wall, and a couple of photos of what appeared to be prep school classmates.

Susan's room, which was just the right size for someone like Lucy with few belongings except for clothes, was neat but soulless, just a place to sleep if she quarreled with her husband. She kept a few odd bits of clothing in the closet and some spare underthings and sweaters in the dresser. All of it could easily be moved out in a box or two if it occurred to Roberta that she couldn't possibly survive without Lucy at her side night and day.

Now she had to think of what to wear tonight, something vaguely glamorous in case Dale did manage to meet her, but also appropriate for dashing downtown to the clubs if he stood her up. She chose a knee-length gauze skirt, black with a few multicolored flowers strewn over it, with a puffy petticoat that made the skirt fluff out like a ballet dancer's tutu; black stockings and soft, low-heeled leather shoes; and a long-sleeved turquoise silk shirt-jacket that seemed perfect for the fall evening. She'd canceled Shakir and her limo for tonight because she'd thought she'd be with Dale. If Dale didn't show up, she'd cab it downtown.

When the phone rang, she answered it without thinking. Margaret hadn't said anything about letting the answering machine pick up the calls. Besides, it might be Dale.

A male voice, but not Dale's, said, "Hi, babe. You going to be in tonight?"

Lucy said, as though he hadn't spoken, "Lady Margaret Priam's residence."

"Sorry," the man said. "I thought Margaret would answer."

"She's out at the moment. This is Lucy Grant. I'm visiting her for a few days. Can I leave her a message? I'll be going out soon, but I can leave her a note." It was getting close to eight.

"If you would. Tell her Sam De Vere called. I'm at home, if she comes in and wants to get back to me."

"I'll do that," Lucy said. So that was the policeman Paul had mentioned, the one who was seeing Margaret and who also shared an apartment with Paul because his mother owned the building and let them live there for free. I wish Carolyn Sue would do that kind of favor for me, she thought, but then she had to dash to make sure the slow elevator in Margaret's building got her down to the street before Dale showed up. It wouldn't do for him not to find her there waiting, even though she half expected not to see him at all.

It had grown cooler between the time she'd left Roberta's place and gone home to change, and her silk shirt was perhaps a little too thin for the night, but she'd be somewhere warmer soon enough. Second Avenue, where the massive tower of Margaret's building stood, was a river of traffic heading downtown, and she wondered where all these people could be going at close to eight o'clock. She peered at the cars that glided past on her side of the avenue, not knowing if Dale would pick her up in a cab or whether he would come in the hired Town Car Roberta said they regularly used when traveling about Manhattan. At least Roberta used it. She said she hated public transportation, but it was much too expensive to maintain a personal car in the city.

Time crept by. He hadn't called her to cancel, and he wasn't the kind of professional who could be called away suddenly from a dinner party for a contrived emergency.

All she could do was pace back and forth for a few more minutes, then flag down a taxi, and go on her way. She was too even-tempered to be angry, but she was human enough to be hurt by the mix-up. And she was hungry.

"Whatever are you doing here on the street?" Margaret had detoured from the direct path to the building to come face-to-face with Lucy.

"I . . . I'm meeting someone, but he seems to be late," Lucy said. "Oh, before I forget, your friend Sam De Vere telephoned. I left you a note. You're to call him back at home. If you want to."

"And I do," Margaret said. "But you shouldn't be hanging around here like a streetwalker. It gives people the wrong impression."

"I'm all right," Lucy said. "I wish people wouldn't worry about me so much."

"If you're sure," Margaret said doubtfully, but she really did want to get to the apartment and call De Vere.

Suddenly a black Lincoln eased up to the curb, the driver got out and opened the back door. Margaret watched Lucy slip into the backseat, but the windows were slightly smoked, so she couldn't see who was in the car. Only a glimpse of a graying male head, and then the door closed and the car wiggled back into the heavy traffic.

Curious, Margaret thought. I could have sworn that was Dale Reeves. No, it's impossible.

But she knew it was not.

Dale pulled Lucy toward him with a fatherly arm around her shoulders. It was a warm and comforting gesture.

"How did you manage to get out of the dinner party?" she asked. "Mrs. Frost was in a dither because there were going to be six extra people for dinner tonight, and I told Roberta to call you to remind you. I didn't think you'd come for me."

"I told a lie," he said, and pulled her closer. Now it was a less fatherly sensation.

"Won't Roberta be angry? What did you tell her? What about your guests?"

"Don't be so concerned about my personal life," Dale said. "I told Roberta that I couldn't get away from some visiting firemen from Europe for a while, dentists here for a seminar. She took it well. Roberta doesn't have the energy to be angry with me. She gets angry with her lady friends who don't perform their duties to her liking, but her interest in me is low enough that she doesn't do more than put on a show when required. But I'm afraid our evening is going to be short, because I do have to show up at a decent hour to make my apologies to our guests. I'll bring her some flowers to make it up to her."

"What will we do, then?" Lucy was so delighted that he had managed to meet her that she didn't really care if Roberta was angry, as long as her name wasn't involved.

"I know a little place where there's a terrific piano player. Not quite the level of a Bobby Short, mind you, but really very good. We can listen to the music, have a drink, and a couple of snacks in case you're hungry. I know I promised you dinner, but you understand. Then I'll drop you back home, and go face the consequences. Okay?"

"It will have to be," Lucy said. She turned the full force of her brilliant smile on him, and was pleased to see his eyes glaze over with something she suspected was lust. She could handle that. They drove in silence for a time over to the West Side. She enjoyed being close to him, perhaps more than she should. "Dale, you'll never tell Roberta that you're taking me out, will you?"

"I may be crazy, but not that crazy."

"But . . . well, people have said that you and . . . and this other woman . . ."

"They're still talking about me and Lorna, are they? She's just a good friend now, although we were very close in the past. I'd like to have you meet her sometime. She'd be a good person to show you the ropes of life in New York."

Lucy pulled away from him a bit. "I don't know why everybody's so worried about hooking me up with people to show me the ropes. Seems to me that New York is just like anyplace else, and besides, I know just about everything there is to know about 'ropes.' I practically grew up with a rope in my hand. And your Susan certainly isn't going to show me anything new."

"You know Susan?"

"Roberta seemed to think that she and I would make a perfect pair of girlfriends in the city. I met her today when she stopped by the apartment, and I can't say I have a high opinion of her."

"Susan is a bit spoiled, I'd say. Her mother's doing. She's never gotten along well with me because she felt I kept her on too short a leash when she was a kid. She and her brother, Gregory, are always fighting about something. In fact, he claims she tried to shoot him once."

"I tried to kill somebody once myself," Lucy said. "Fortunately, I failed."

"I can't imagine a sweet thing like you having murderous thoughts. Who was it?"

"Just a girl who tried to break up my relationship with my boyfriend Filipe. His sister Consuela. She didn't like seeing a Latino and an Anglo going together. Those Garcia sisters are tough, but I did manage to get her on the ground and cut off her hair before Filipe separated us and took away my knife." Lucy laughed. "You should have seen her. She was so proud of her long, black hair."

"Families are funny things," Dale said. "Greg and I have had our rough patches. I wanted him to follow in my footsteps and go to dental school, but he wouldn't hear of it. Still, both kids like having a place in Manhattan that they don't pay for, where they can drop in and inconvenience us at will. Here we are."

The club was small and dark, with only a pale spotlight on the piano player, a young black man wearing a white jacket. Each of the little round tables surrounding the piano had a candle on it. Several people were there listening to the music, but the place wasn't packed.

Dale scanned the room. "Nobody here I know. Good. There won't be any gossip floating around about seeing me here with an attractive young woman who's not my wife."

"Does that worry you?"

He shrugged. "Not much. We're not doing anything wrong. It's just that if Roberta hears something and figures out I was here with you when I should have been home with our guests, she might get the wrong idea."

"But she doesn't get angry with you."

"That might just do it. Come on, order a drink and listen to this guy. He's terrific." He ordered some Buffalo chicken wings, and cocktail shrimp. Lucy drank white wine, which she had quickly learned was the proper choice for New York damsels, even though she'd grown up drinking tequila and beer with her Mexican friends, and a bit of bourbon with her father's friends.

While the pianist played Cole Porter, she asked Dale, "What's this all about, anyhow?"

"What's 'this'?"

"You and me. I'm just a kid compared to you, and I don't have, oh, sophistication or wit or even vaguely common interests with you."

"I liked you the minute I saw you," he said. "You're a beautiful girl, and maybe I'm just exploring whether there are common interests, sophistication to be uncovered, or wit that will bloom suddenly in this dark, old room."

"Or maybe you just want to get back at your wife for reasons I don't know and don't want to know. That's not fair to me, you know." She looked at him. "I might decide that I care a lot for you. And I could end up losing my job if your wife catches on, just when I'm beginning to learn something. Roberta's pretty amazing. She's very disorganized, but she has power. She can tell those women what to do, and they do it. I want to be able to do the same thing, only I'd keep everything in perfect order, and everything would get done on time."

"You're a smart kid, Lucy, even if you don't think you're witty or sophisticated. I couldn't agree more about Roberta, but with all she does, there isn't much time left for me. We used to travel a lot, seeing all kinds of wonderful places. We used to take cruises to places like Alaska and the Caribbean at least once a year, but not anymore. She has too many commitments to take the time. We used to go to the theatre weekly, just the two of us, and not as part of some gala fund-raising event. We'd entertain our friends and not a bunch of committee members and their husbands. So now I play golf to occupy my free time." He looked at his watch. "I'd better take you back and then head home if I'm going to keep what friends I have. I'm sorry. I wanted it to be a fun night."

"Just the fact that you arranged to come has made it fun," she said. "I mean, I knew you would, but still, I guess I thought you wouldn't. I do understand that you have obligations that don't include me. And don't worry about taking me home. I'll go across town a little way and stop in at one of the clubs. Lots of fun people there, and I'll take a cab home. I'll be okay. You hurry along so you won't be too late for your guests."

They parted in the street, Lucy refusing his offer to drop her at the club. He wouldn't leave, though, until he'd flagged down a cab for her. At the cab's door, he kissed her gently on the cheek, and closed the door behind her.

She watched him get into the Town Car as the taxi took her away, and shook her head. What was that all about, she wondered. It made her feel really good to think he'd risk Roberta's wrath just to take her out as he'd promised, but much as she liked the romantic gesture, she wondered if it was worth it. Men are nuts, she decided, and they'll make you nuts, too, if you let them. But at least Dale was good-natured and kind, and he wouldn't be so bad to live with for years and years. With his importance and her money, she could take over the roles Roberta filled so haphazardly, and have the kind of life that would please Carolyn Sue. She wasn't so sure that Margaret would willingly give her approval.

She decided she needed a plan. One was beginning to form as the taxi carried her through the night.

Chapter 13

Lucy Rose's heart wasn't in clubland after all. She looked in at one place, wasn't thrilled by what she saw, although she did spot Frankie with a bunch of his friends. She didn't want to talk to him tonight, so she left after a few minutes and went home. Margaret was again out, perhaps with her boyfriend, De Vere. Lucy was glad that somebody was having a good time. Margaret had left her a note saying that if she could get free of Roberta for an hour or so the next day, a real estate person who worked for Carolyn Sue wanted to show her an apartment.

Lucy felt so claustrophobic in her tiny bedroom that she'd make time to look for a place of her own. Still, the idea of Susan's room in the Reeves' apartment had captured her fancy. She could be there with Dale all the time. She could bring him a drink or something at bedtime, and see him off to his office in the morning. When Roberta was out in the evenings with her committees, she and Dale could watch TV or go out to dinner without feeling like they were sneaking around. Bliss. Best of all, she'd be able to do all the organizing for Dale's birthday party. It wouldn't even matter if Roberta approved or not. It would be like planning a party in her own home, the way she used to back in Dallas. Not even Mrs. Frost could prevent her from using the kitchen if she actually lived there. And she was certain that Margaret wouldn't mind at all seeing her leave. The key was getting Susan to give up her space in her mother's apartment willingly. And that could only happen if Roberta told her to leave. She'd worry about that tomorrow.

Little Lucia Rose went to sleep remembering Dale Reeves' gentle kiss on her cheek on a dingy street on the West Side of Manhattan. She dreamed of the flickering candles on the little tables and the background music that was all Cole Porter, so different from the noisy rap and pop songs the DJs played at the clubs. She slept well.

"Did you get to see your boyfriend last night?" Lucy noticed that Margaret seemed especially cheerful the next morning as she brewed coffee and poured the orange juice.

"Yes, finally. He's been out of town. You got in before me, I see."

"The fun of the clubs can wear off pretty fast," Lucy said.

"You didn't take your usual limo, I noticed. Who was that who picked you up? I hope you knew him."

"Oh, yes." Lucy wouldn't meet Margaret's eye. "Just a friend."

Margaret knew she was about to shift into her old auntie role in the next sentence. "Lucy, I don't really know how things are done in Texas. I mean, it may be perfectly acceptable for a girl like you to, say, date the father of one of your friends. But given the work you've taken on, and the people involved, if you want to be accepted in the social circles that Carolyn Sue seems to think you're suited for, I would suggest that you be very, very careful to avoid a situation you can't really handle. If the women who matter decided to stand up against you, you wouldn't stand a chance. And I am talking about Roberta Reeves. I don't think she'd condone a romance between her assistant and her husband, however 'understanding' she's been about Lorna. There, that's all I have to say on the matter, although I'd be glad to talk further if you wish. It's your choice."

"We haven't done anything wrong, really. He just took me out for a little while to hear this wonderful piano player. That's all." Although Margaret didn't know the girl well enough to recognize it, Lucy's father would certainly recognize her stubborn look and understand its meaning: Nobody was going to tell Lucia Rose what to do.

"I still beg you to go carefully," Margaret said. "It wouldn't do me or Carolyn Sue any good either if we were associated with a scandal like that when you're our responsibility." Margaret actually didn't give a fig for what people thought, and she believed Lucy when she said there was nothing to it. Yet, with people like Audrey Cheever already assuming that Lucy's raison d'être was to be part of Roberta's diabolical plan to interfere with Dale's relationship with poor Lorna Hutchison, a plan that Lucy was probably unaware of, Lucy had better tread very carefully indeed.

"I told you about Dale's birthday party, didn't I?" Margaret nodded. "Well, Mrs. Frost, the cook, is almost willing to allow me into her kitchen to make barbecue. Now all I have to do is tell Roberta about it, and we're on our way."

"What if she objects?"

"Mrs. Frost says that nobody ever remembers his birthday, and his son doesn't treat him very well, so I'm sure I can get Roberta to believe that she thought up the whole idea herself. And, guess what, I'm going to ask Roberta if I can have Susan's bedroom. She only comes around now and then; she and her husband have a home of their own somewhere out of the city. It's not fair for her to take up all that space when someone else really needs it. Anyhow, I have a plan. . . ."

But she didn't tell Margaret about her plan. She just grabbed her handbag and dashed away. Margaret shook her head. She had the feeling that something unpleasant was going to come of all this. Lucy was back in a minute. "Even if I can persuade Roberta to get rid of her daughter, I'd still better take a look at that apartment you mentioned. I'll call you when I've cleared a long lunch hour with Roberta."

"I'll be here," Margaret said, vaguely uncomfortable still about the connection between Richard Centner and Roberta, and now Lucy, who was in her way connected with Roberta's husband, not to mention her daughter. Whoever said that New York was a town full of strangers certainly didn't know this bunch. You practically tripped over someone's nearest and dearest at every street corner.

Happily for Margaret, her dear friend Dianne Stark had returned from Los Angeles, and the two of them were going to have lunch in a day or two, complete with some good old gossip. At least Margaret had tales to tell, and Dianne was never one to repeat anything, so the story of Lucy's adventures could be examined and discussed without fear of it reaching the ears of others.

Dianne had risen to a high social level by marrying a wealthy man who doted on her and who had only one, slightly troublesome, former wife. Dianne and Charlie were the parents of a lively little boy, and although there had been a rough patch a while back involving Dianne's sister, things seemed to have settled down again for the Starks.

After determining that the empty life of a society dame was the road to ruin, Dianne was actually about to start training to be a caregiver for disabled persons.

"Not a real nurse," she told Margaret. "I don't think I could handle the academic side. I had a hard enough time passing exams when I was a teenager. But I think I can learn what's necessary to help those poor folks live something like a normal life." She was so sincere about her plans that Margaret almost felt that she should join her. After all, Margaret had a child from a long-ago marriage who had been disabled and had died young. Maybe it was time for her to make herself really useful to society, not Society.

To Margaret's surprise, Poppy Dill was calling her, instead of the other way around. "I spoke to your young friend Lucia Rose yesterday," Poppy said. "She seemed like quite a nice young woman. Wanted publicity for one of Roberta's events, but she asked politely and all that. I think manners are so important, and so few of the younger set seem to know what I'm talking about. I liked her. So I'm putting in the item about her in tomorrow's column. She should be getting a lot of play from it in the next few days. Everybody reads me, and everybody wants to be the first to take up a new face."

"I'm sure she'll appreciate that," Margaret said. "Only . . . well, I was having my hair done at Norman's the other day at the same time as Audrey Cheever, and Audrey was spouting the most terrible nonsense, about how people are saying that Lucy was recruited by Roberta to take Dale Reeves' attention away from Lorna. Roberta had planned it all. It can't be true, can it?"

"I don't think Roberta thinks that far ahead. I mean, look at the way she organizes her benefits. But there is something curious," Poppy said. "Only this morning, one of my . . . um . . . informants called to say that Dale Reeves had been spotted in some dive over on the West Side with an amazingly attractive young woman, dark hair, dark brows. Really striking. The informant was there because he covers up-and-coming artists for my newspaper, and this club, or whatever it is, has a piano player who's supposed to be really something. Michael Feinstein and Bobby rolled into one, with a few other added delights. The man knows Dale, perhaps professionally, although how he can afford a dentist of Dale's price range I don't know. Anyhow, he made the identification." Poppy paused for breath, or at least to think how to phrase what was coming next. "The thing is, my friend also covers a lot of minor general news, including some international dental convention being held in New York. Dale was supposed to be a speaker last evening, but he didn't show, so the organizers called his home and were told that he was out with people from that very convention. All the while he was canoodling in the dark with some young thing."

"Just between us, Poppy, it was Lucy Rose. She told me all about it. So now Roberta must know that something is up, even if she doesn't know it was Lucy. Well, let's hope she thinks it was Lorna, although she doesn't fit the description. Let's hope Dale denies everything. I don't want Lucy to get into deep trouble."

"My lips are sealed, as usual," Poppy said. "You

know me. There's so much I know that will never be made public." Margaret could tell that she was thrilled to have some juicy gossip that she certainly wouldn't tell, but she could let on to others that she knew far more that she was not telling. It was all part of the Poppy persona, like the reluctance to venture out of her apartment, and the manual typewriter she still used, only transferring her copy to the computer linked to the newspaper's offices under stern threats from her employers.

"I'm constantly afraid that Lucy is going to get herself into trouble," Margaret said. "If only she'd meet a nice single boy from a good family and become enamored of him."

"I wouldn't count on that," Poppy said. "Most of the nice boys I know about are either not so nice or are engaged or married already. There's only Paul who's still reasonably available, and even he's half spoken for. Margaret, you don't think this thing with Dale is serious, do you?"

"Probably not from Lucy's side, but I'm not sure I understand the minds of middle-aged men. Dale's coming up on his fiftieth birthday. He may be trying to recapture his youth. I hear it happens quite a lot."

"It does," Poppy said, "although why these men think that shedding a loyal wife of many years to take on a young woman who could be their daughter is the road to eternal youth, I haven't the slightest idea. But they will do it. Oh, I could tell you tales. . . ." And then proceeded to do so, until Margaret was sure she could never look at a man over fifty again without thinking of the escapades that Poppy had described in lurid detail.

"I'm seeing Dianne soon, on Sunday perhaps," Margaret said, when Poppy had run out of stories. "She starts her training next week, so this will be the last chance for a while for us to be ladies of leisure, free to lunch at all the best places."

"Such a dear girl," Poppy said. "And so clever to have landed Charlie. Who was, I might note, a middle-aged man who dropped one wife for a younger version. They seem to have worked everything out successfully. I suppose all Charlie's money was helpful. Keep me posted on Lucy Rose."

"I will," Margaret said, "although I fervently hope that there is nothing to keep you posted about. At least there's no madman running around with a gun, for once."

"But there may be a madwoman," Poppy said knowingly, and rang off.

Chapter 14

"*You're a bit late* today," Roberta said snappishly when Lucy walked in. She didn't respond, because it was in fact only eight-thirty, exactly the time she'd arrived every day in the past.

"How was your dinner party?" Lucy couldn't help asking as she started to pull papers relating to urgent tasks from their various folders.

"Disaster, start to finish. Dale got caught up in some kind of thing with visiting professors of dentistry, so I had to deal with a bunch of people I scarcely knew, until he bothered to show up. It worked out in the end, and Dale was so apologetic that nobody could complain. And he brought me some lovely flowers. I think that shows some kind of consideration."

Lucy breathed a sigh of relief that her name hadn't figured at all, and she bent to her work.

"I'm going to have to run out for an hour for another quick fitting. It's just over on Madison, so I won't be gone long. Dale has left and Mrs. Frost is out. Carlotta isn't feeling well, so she's keeping to her room for today. If the doorman rings, find out who it is, and have them call back later when I'm home. If it's somebody delivering something, have the doorman hold it until I return.

I don't want you answering the door to strangers when there's nobody else around."

"I'll be right here," Lucy said, but as soon as she heard Roberta depart, she moved into the hall and made her way carefully toward the large formal dining room. She was getting on with her plan, thanks to Mrs. Frost.

The gorgeous Georgian silver tea service was displayed proudly on a polished mahogany sideboard. Lucy used the edge of her jacket to pick up the lovely silver creamer, which she carried to the room that was assigned to Susan. She carefully opened a drawer of the dresser, and hid the creamer under a pile of sensible cotton undergarments that Susan had stored there.

She was busy making lists in the drawing room when Roberta returned from her fitting. "It's going to be a lovely dress, the most beautiful shade of red," she said. "I plan to wear it at the hospital benefit."

"Will I be expected to attend? If I am, I'll need to find something to wear myself." She knew she had brought plenty of suitable dresses with her from Texas. "I don't care one way or the other, but I want to be prepared."

"Of course you can come, if you like. They're pretty boring affairs, though, if you don't know everybody. I've asked Susan and her husband to join us, but they don't really care for this sort of party."

"Susan didn't mention anything about it when she dropped by yesterday," Lucy said.

"Susan was here? You didn't tell me."

"I didn't think to mention it. She stayed just a few minutes. Mrs. Frost said something about the tea service, although I don't remember just what it was."

"Susan loves those pieces, although I doubt that she has any idea what they're worth. They belonged to my grandmother. Susan will inherit them one day, unless we have to sell the whole set off. That's what antiques are good for, a bit of ready cash when times get tough."

Suddenly Roberta grew restless and began to pace, distracting Lucy.

"I think I'll see if Mrs. Frost has any ginger ale," Roberta said, and left the room. She was gone for quite a while. When she returned, her face was red with fury. "Since Mrs. Frost is out and Carlotta is indisposed, I want you to come with me while I look for something. I want a witness."

Roberta marched out of the room, with Lucy following. They made their way through the apartment to the door of Susan's room. "She used to keep it locked until I put my foot down," Roberta said. "After all, it is *my* apartment, filled with *my* belongings. Just stand there; don't touch anything, but come when I call you." Roberta started with the shelves in the closet, then moved to the bed, feeling under the pillows and mattress. Finally she reached the dresser and started opening the drawers. Lucy heard her gasp when she touched the hard creamer under the pile of panties.

"Come here now, and watch me while I remove these things." Roberta shoved the clothing aside to reveal the creamer. "What is it they say about a serpent's tooth? Look here, look very carefully. I want you to be able to swear that you saw me find this creamer in Susan's drawer. Well, do you swear to it?"

"Yes, ma'am," Lucy said with a tremble in her voice, but a smile in her heart. "I saw you find it. What does it mean?"

"It means that Susan has a lot to answer for," Roberta

said grimly. "Now, do I leave it here, or put it back where it belongs?"

"I wouldn't leave it here," Lucy said. "She might come back and take it away. That must have been what she was planning to do, although I don't know why she didn't take it yesterday. I wouldn't have known."

"Back it goes to the dining room," Roberta said, "and the whole tea service goes into storage as soon as Mrs. Frost gets home. And Lucy, for your help in this matter, what would you think of taking this room and living here with us? I don't want to lay eyes on Susan ever again. We have so much room, and it's a pity to see it all go to waste."

"I think that would be lovely, Roberta. I'd like so much to have a nice big room like this. And I'll be right here to help you every minute of the day and night. Oh, that reminds me, Margaret wants me to take a long lunch hour so I can look at an apartment that Carolyn Sue has lined up for me."

"You don't have to do that now," Roberta said. "Everything's settled."

"Then I'd better call Margaret right away. Mr. Centner is expecting to meet us."

"Wait," Roberta said. "Is that Richard Centner?"

Lucy shrugged. "I can't remember his first name. Could be."

"Why don't you call Margaret and have the two of them meet you here. It might be a good idea if you had an alternate place, in case you don't like living here."

"I'd much rather be here with you, Roberta." For a minute she wondered if living here would be as much of a joy as she'd thought. Sure, Dale would be close by, and she wouldn't have to worry about paying rent, but she suspected the arrangement would bring a halt to her ventures into the city's nightlife, and she certainly couldn't bring Frankie and the other guys here. Then she shrugged off her concern. Nobody was going to tell her what to do, and if she wanted to stay out all night, it was nobody's business but her own. She could handle Roberta Reeves. And Dale Reeves. Maybe soon enough she would be in charge here, and then surely nobody could tell her anything.

She called Margaret at once, to catch her before she went out. "Margaret, guess what. Roberta has invited me to stay here at her apartment. She's kicking her daughter out because she stole some valuable family silver. I won't need to look at apartments, after all, and I'll be out of your hair in a couple of days, after the kicking out is finished. That should be something to hear. Susan is not a nice person."

"All right," Margaret said. "I'll call Richard Centner and tell him the appointment is off."

"Well, the thing is, Roberta thinks I should look at apartments anyhow, in case I'm not happy here. She wants you and Mr. Centner to meet me here."

"I see," Margaret said. "I guess that can be arranged. It's possible that Roberta will work things out with Susan, and restore her to her room. You never know what people are going to do."

Susan, in fact, was furious. Lucy couldn't help overhearing the shrieks that came from the telephone when Roberta called her daughter and instructed her to remove her belongings from the "guest room" she'd taken over, even though she had a perfectly good home of her own.

"Please be sure not to take anything that doesn't belong to you," Roberta said. "You know what I'm talking about. Lucy and I found the creamer in the dresser drawer," she said to her daughter and then turned again to Lucy.

"She said she absolutely didn't know what I was talking about, and if she ever does have a baby, I will never, ever see my grandchild," Roberta said. She looked so tired and unhappy that Lucy put her arm around her and patted her gently.

"It will be all right, Roberta. She did something foolish, but of course she'd deny it. I'm sure she'll make amends. You'll see. A few months from now, you won't even remember this."

"You're such a comfort, Lucy. I almost wish you were my daughter, instead of Susan."

"Well, it will seem that way if I'm to be living here."

"Maybe Dale ought to convince Greg that he should empty out his room, too. It's really not right for a grown man to expect his father to pay for all that expensive space. He's not here more than once a year, if that. It might make Susan feel less upset if her brother got the same treatment as she did. Even though I will never forget that she stole from me. Never."

Lucy was curious to see the man that people said had romanced Roberta, so she listened for his and Margaret's arrival around noon. After hastily canceling a luncheon date, Roberta had retired to her room to change her clothes and repair her makeup.

Lucy expected a dreamboat, but what she found was a fairly ordinary looking man, nicely dressed, but hardly an instant object of passion. Roberta made a grand entrance.

"Rich, how good to see you after all this time. You're looking well. . . ." Roberta uttered the usual flattering nonsense, to which, alas, Rich did not respond in kind. Roberta was not pleased to see her hopes of rekindling a relationship gently dashed.

"I've thought about you often," she said, "and I almost called you last month, just to hear your voice. After what we were to each other . . ." She didn't seem to care that Margaret and Lucy were listening to every word.

"I would have been glad to hear from you, of course," Centner said. "But don't go thinking we can start over. It was finished a long time ago, and I've moved on with my life."

Roberta was pale, and she fiddled nervously with her rings. Lucy noticed they were old-looking hands, and she almost felt sorry for her employer, whose husband was half-infatuated with Lucy, whose old beau was rejecting her firmly.

"I suppose we ought to get moving," Centner said, "if I'm going to show the young lady an apartment or two. Have to do my best for Carolyn Sue."

They left a deflated Roberta, and walked to the cross street off Lexington, where Carolyn Sue had acquired her latest buildings.

"She's never given up," Centner said. "Poor gal. She doesn't understand that when flings are finished, they're finished for good."

"I don't think we need to know this," Margaret said. "It's really private business between the two of you. Is this the building? It looks nice."

Lucy examined the apartments without interest. In her mind, she was settled in Susan's room, and that was that.

In fact, Susan sent a woman and a man that very afternoon to pack up the few things in her room, since she refused to set foot in the apartment until her mother apologized for accusing her of theft.

Lucy mentally crossed Susan's name off the guest list for Dale's birthday party, but she thought she had Roberta softened up enough to propose her party idea.

"Ah, Roberta, I noticed that Dr. Reeves' birthday is coming up."

"Is it the middle of September already? I guess you're right. I never remember it," Roberta said. "How did you know about it?"

"I guess he must have mentioned it. Wouldn't it be fun to have a surprise party for him? Right here, I mean, out on the terrace. You have that beautiful space and you never seem to use it. I was feeling a little homesick for Texas and started thinking about barbecue and stuff; and then I thought, if there were only a reason to throw a party, not a big charity event, but a kind of family thing. Oh, please, let's do it."

"You young people. Here you are organizing—with me, of course—three major parties, and you want to do still another one." But Roberta was smiling, so Lucy knew she had won. "It will definitely surprise Dale to think that I remembered his birthday and went to all the trouble of making a party for him."

"You can do it," Lucy said. "It's the perfect timing in the middle of all the other ones. It won't interfere at all."

"Then let's do it," Roberta said gaily. "I think it will be fun, and best of all, there won't be any committee meetings to attend."

"Oh, no," Lucy said. "I'll handle everything."

Chapter 15

"*I'm staying in tonight,*" Lucy told Margaret. "I want to start getting packed for my move to the Reeves' apartment. I should be able to finish up over the weekend, and move in on Sunday."

Margaret was planning to cook bluefish at De Vere's apartment that evening, since Paul had gone away for the weekend, so she was perfectly content to let Lucy drag her clothes out of the shared closet and pack them into suitcases without her assistance.

"I'll bet you're pleased to have livable space, for a change," Margaret said.

"And when they get rid of Greg Reeves from the other room, I can probably talk Roberta into letting me have that one as well. It's a perfect setup. And by the way, Roberta thinks the birthday party is a great idea. We're going to do it. You'll come, won't you? And bring your boyfriend, and Paul?"

"I think it's supposed to be Dale's party, not yours," Margaret said. "Well, if Roberta approves of my name on the guest list, I'll come, but I won't promise Sam. He's highly allergic to parties that occur on Park Avenue. I suppose Paul could be considered your date, so Roberta probably won't object to him, especially considering who his mother is."

"Everything is working out perfectly," Lucy said, but Margaret wondered if her expression signified true contentment or mere smugness.

Just to uphold her unwanted role as guidance counselor and mentor, Margaret said, "I really would be careful about getting too involved with Dale Reeves, Lucy. It could lead to trouble along the way."

But Lucy didn't answer. Instead, she conveyed an armload of outfits, still on their hangers, from Margaret's closet to the open suitcases in her bedroom.

"People saw you and Dale out together last night. And people will spread gossip, no matter how innocent you think your behavior was." At least Margaret could be almost certain that Poppy wouldn't spread the word. She was very good about keeping secrets if you asked her nicely.

"I don't have any plans to go anywhere with him again soon," Lucy said. "But I can't avoid him in his own apartment, can I?"

"Maybe you ought to consider an apartment of your own," Margaret said. "The ones Rich Centner showed you were perfectly fine. I'll call him anytime you like."

"Don't like," Lucy said in a stubborn voice. "It's all settled." If Margaret had known her better, she would have understood that when Lucy Rose turned stubborn, there was nothing to be done, not even by the strong-willed Big Ed.

"Do you think José would help me carry this stuff to the Reeves' place on Sunday if I slipped him a few dollars?"

"I'm sure he would be delighted," Margaret said. "He

usually works on the weekends, but I'm not sure the building manager would allow him to take time off to cart your belongings elsewhere in the city."

"I can arrange it," Lucy said. "I'm sure the building manager is open to a small gratuity for doing me a favor."

Margaret wasn't so sure. The manager was a constantly harried individual who had to deal with favors demanded by a very large population of residents.

"Anyhow, José must have a lunch hour, or a little free time after work or before it. It won't take long. All I can do is ask."

"I'm leaving now," Margaret said. "I have to pick up a few things for tonight." She was eager to get away from Lucy and packing and José. "I guess tomorrow will be almost our last breakfast together. It's been fun."

Lucy looked at her oddly. It hadn't been all that much fun, and they both knew it.

"I've got to call Carolyn Sue," she told De Vere when she arrived at the apartment in Chelsea. It was a charming duplex with a little garden in back, and there was plenty of room so that De Vere and Paul seldom had to encounter each other on the rare occasions when both were in residence.

"Go right ahead," De Vere said "Carolyn Sue pays the phone bill, so she won't mind one more call."

After Margaret had gotten past an inquisitive servant who answered the phone, Carolyn Sue came on the line. Apparently, there was some sort of gathering taking place, because she was backed by noisy voices.

"What's happenin' up there in New York?"

"More to the point, what's happening there? I can scarcely hear you."

"Just some folks who came by to welcome me back. I tell you, they sure do miss little me when I leave town for a few days. Let me take this call in the study, where it's quieter."

Put on hold, Margaret poked about in Paul's kitchen. Evidently Carolyn Sue had ensured that her boy had everything he could possibly need in the way of cooking utensils, or else Paul was more of a gourmet cook than she had imagined. The bluefish fillets were nearly defrosted, and she had sent De Vere to the garden to shuck the ears of corn he had brought from Connecticut.

Carolyn Sue returned. "Is there trouble?" she asked.

"Not exactly. Were you expecting trouble?"

"I've learned never to take things for granted when Lucy Rose is involved. Big Ed'll tell you the same thing, in less polite terms. Rich Centner called me and told me she'd made some kind of living arrangements that didn't include one of my apartments. What's that all about?"

"She's moving into a room at the Reeves' apartment. Now that would be fine under normal circumstances, but it seems that she's been going out and about with Dale, and they've been seen. Even Poppy has heard about it, although so far, Roberta apparently hasn't. I don't think she should be staying right there with Dale and Roberta, but she refuses to look at the apartments Rich Centner has lined up. I have no status with her, and I can't control what she does. I was wondering if . . ."

"If Carolyn Sue would ride to the rescue? I can do that, honey. I was thinkin' I ought to come to New York anyhow to see how Richie is handlin' my business. He doesn't have the best reputation, especially after him and

Peter Anton went bust over the house of Peter's wife. You just hang in there for a couple of days, and I'll be there to talk some sense into the girl. Lordy, Margaret, I was sure blessed to have a son like Paul instead of a daughter like Lucy. Worst Paul has done is not doin' so well with the jobs Ben finds for him, and maybe spendin' a little too much money on high livin' in Europe. 'Course, that's my fault. I gave it to him, but I've mended my ways, thanks to Ben.''

"Thanks," Margaret said. "I knew you'd help."

She grilled the bluefish and boiled the corn gently, tossed a salad and set the table.

"You'll be happy to know that your favorite rich lady will soon be arriving," she told De Vere when they sat down to eat. "Yes, luv, Carolyn Sue is flying in to the rescue of my misguided former houseguest." She told him about Lucy's dangerous forays into the night with a married man, the husband of her employer, and how the story was certain to get about. De Vere had minimal interest in the sins of the upper classes, unless someone got murdered and Margaret found herself involved. Then he could become quite stern and concerned.

"This Lucy is just a kid," he said. "She has to make her own mistakes, but she seems capable of getting herself out of trouble." Then De Vere made it clear that they had reached the end of any further discussion about Lucy Rose. "But I'll be glad to see Carolyn Sue. Did she mention whether she's planning on staying here with us?"

"Surely she'll stay at the Villa d'Este, so she won't have any housekeeping chores." The idea of Carolyn Sue Castrocani Hoopes dipping her diamond-laden fingers into soapy dishwater or wielding a vacuum cleaner, decked out in Prada, amused Margaret and De Vere, and they passed some happy moments retelling tales of Carolyn Sue.

Back at Margaret's apartment, Lucy finished her packing quickly, and found herself in the early evening with nothing to do. She contemplated an excursion into clubland once again. She hadn't yet visited the Tunnel, which everybody said was a wild place for wild—even dangerous—fun. With Margaret away for the evening, she even contemplated inviting Dale to come around to visit her. Not a good idea, she decided. Roberta might answer the phone if she called, or Carlotta might recognize her voice asking for Dale.

About nine, however, the intercom from the lobby buzzed.

"A gentleman to see Miss Grant," the doorman said.

"And who would he be?" Lucy asked.

There was a sort of mumbled conversation in the lobby, and the doorman said, "Mr. Gregory Reeves."

Lucy shrugged to herself. She'd never met him, but why not? She could hope he wasn't as unpleasant as his sister. "Have him come up," she said. She checked her appearance in a mirror, but she wasn't worried. She always looked good. She wasn't wearing anything really nice, but she didn't think it mattered.

Greg Reeves turned out to be a rather hunky number. He looked a bit like his father, but better, and of course, much younger.

"Really an unexpected pleasure," she said as she let him in. She noticed that he was serious and unsmiling. "Do sit down. Can I offer you something? Not that I'm sure there's anything to offer. I'm just a temporary guest here."

"I don't need anything," Greg said. He sat there not saying anything, but looking her over covertly. "Um . . . Miss Grant, I don't quite know where to begin. My father and I don't always get along, but we're pretty close most of the time, and sometimes we even confide in each other. Roberta has never been much of a loving mother, and Susan is simply a top-quality bitch who hates my guts. That being said, I hope you understand that I don't really care about their happiness. On the other hand, my parents have a pretty solid marriage and Roberta appears to make Dad happy, and I do care about that. When he strays, she gets very angry and makes life hell for him. He ends up being not happy. I don't want that to happen. Do you understand me?"

"What is there to understand?" Lucy said. "People do what they have to do, whether it's your parents or your sister or anybody else."

"I've heard, from my father as well as others, that you've been seeing him, while you're working for his wife."

"Oh, not really. He took me to lunch once, and out to hear some music. I don't count that as 'seeing' someone."

"Now I hear that you're planning to move into the apartment. I don't know how Susan managed to rile up Roberta, but she's furious, and she's kicked Susan out of her bedroom away from home, so you can use it."

"She stole something from her mother," Lucy said. "I was there when Roberta found it hidden in a dresser."

"I don't believe that Susan needed to steal anything from Mother, but I really don't like the idea of you thinking you can steal Dale from her."

Lucy put on her best, her most dazzling smile. "That's nonsense. I have no intention . . ."

"I'm not asking you what your feelings or intentions are. But I do understand from what he's said that my father is quite taken with you. I want it stopped, right now. I don't want you moving into the apartment, and if necessary, I'll expect you to quit your job with Roberta."

She smiled again and said, "And I expect you'll be leaving now, Mr. Reeves. But I do hope you're coming to your father's surprise birthday party in a week. Surprise, remember. Don't spoil it for Roberta, or Dale."

He left quietly, which did surprise her. She had expected more threats and pleas. She was also a bit surprised that Dale had talked about her with his son, but she supposed guys liked to share stories of their conquests with other guys, just the way she and Tyler Anne did. After he was gone, she decided how she was going to take care of Gregory Reeves. Then she picked up the phone.

"Carlotta, it's Lucy. I have to speak to Dr. Reeves immediately. It's an emergency, but don't alarm Mrs. Reeves." She tried to put a few tears into her voice.

"She's gone out," Carlotta said. "I think the doctor is here. You keep calm." Carlotta had a heavy Spanish accent, and could sometimes feign ignorance of English, but she rose to the bait.

"What's the matter?" Dale came to the phone promptly. "Carlotta says there's trouble."

While she waited for him, Lucy had been summoning up a fit of broken breathing and the hint of hysteria, so she was ready for him. "Dale, Dale, it's Gregory. He . . . He came here to Margaret's apartment. She's away tonight. Of course I let him in because he's your son. I had no idea . . ." She had worked herself up to a point where the act had almost become reality. "I don't know him, I never met him, but he . . . he attacked me. I managed to get away from him before anything happened. He tried to tear my clothes off and . . . and . . ." Now she was really crying. She could always bring up a few tears when she thought about the time her absolute favorite gelding had broken its leg and had to be put down.

"But you're all right? I'll be there in ten minutes, no, five. What could Greg have been thinking? Listen, sweetheart, don't let anybody in but me. Promise?"

Sniff, sniff. Sob, sob. "I promise. Please hurry." Little Lucy Rose wiped away her tears. She put a hot, wet washcloth on her face so she would appear flushed, darkened the area under her eyes, and ripped the sleeve of her blouse, fortunately one of her least favorite ones.

All right, Mr. Gregory Reeves, she thought. Let's just see what your expectations are now.

Chapter 16

"*What could* have gotten into Greg to do such a thing? Look, he tore your shirt. But he barely knew about you. I may have mentioned your name to him, and told him you were working with Roberta and staying with Lady Margaret, but he could have no reason to come here and attempt to molest you." Dale Reeves shook his head sadly. "He's not a violent person, and as far as I know, he and Melissa are a perfectly happy couple. Oh, the usual spats, but he's never looked at another woman."

"I don't think I can ever go back to your apartment, on the chance that he might be there."

"Don't worry, he won't be welcome in my home, not after this. First Susan and now Greg. I'm beginning to think there's insanity in the family."

"Did you . . . did you mention to him that you and I . . ."

"We're just friends, Lucy. Oh, I may have mentioned that you were a real pretty little thing, but I never suggested anything more."

"But maybe he imagined more. Like I would welcome his attentions. Men can be awfully strange sometimes. I remember once when I was in college, this guy I barely knew actually kidnapped me and took me to New

Hampshire. He wrote a ransom note to my father and everything. And I never did a thing to make him think I wanted that. We were just talking at a party about how awful human beings are to the environment, and suddenly it was like he owned me."

"Don't think about it. But you know, the only charity gala I ever enjoyed going to, felt was worthwhile, was one my wife chaired to save the rain forests. I give a lot of money to environmental causes myself. I'm not sure I'd kidnap you for them, however."

Lucy was curled up on the sofa close to Dale, gazing at him with those lovely thick-lashed eyes. "I do worry about the environment a lot. Did you know that the songbirds are vanishing because their habitat is disappearing? I can't imagine a world without birdsong in the morning. I even turned down Daddy's offer of a mink jacket because I couldn't stand the idea of killing those dear little animals," she told him with a straight face. The truth was, Lucia Rose had often heard Carolyn Sue state her belief that there were far too many minks in the world, and their highest calling was to keep the likes of Mrs. Ben Hoopes warm and fashionable. Lucy tended to agree.

In fact, Lucy had lost out on the mink jacket because Big Ed had chanced to find her drinking margaritas in a dingy bar with Filipe and some other Mexican boys who had been caught trying to steal a television set from his house. After she explained to Big Ed that she'd invited the boys home and had told them her family had way too many TV sets, so why not take one, Big Ed had been mightily displeased. Finding her continuing to consort with them meant the end of the mink jacket. Pure bad timing, not the desire to save helpless animals or the environment, was to blame.

"Poor Lucy," Dale crooned. "I'd love to buy you a mink jacket, but I think I'll do something even better. Something you'll really appreciate. I'll insist that Roberta get rid of her mink coat and sable jacket."

"She'll be furious," Lucy said. She'd seen the Maximilian sable, and it was gorgeous.

"She'll have to learn to live with it," Dale said. "I have to make up for what Greg did."

"I know a way you could make it up," Lucy said.

"All you have to do is ask, sweetheart."

"Well, if I'm going to have Susan's room, it will be absolutely filled with my clothes, and I sort of need more space to relax in, you know, watch television and read, maybe invite my girlfriends to visit. I wouldn't want to disturb you and Roberta if you were entertaining. So maybe it would be a good idea if Greg moved his stuff out, and I took that room, too. I'd have the bath between the two rooms all to myself, and it would almost be like my own apartment. I'd take care of both rooms myself, so Carlotta wouldn't have any extra work."

"I don't see why it can't be arranged," Dale said. "In fact, it's a great idea. And don't worry about overworking Carlotta. She spends far too much time lying down, as it is. Look, I ought to get home to bed. Early appointment tomorrow. On the golf course. My rich patients don't like Sunday appointments. Will you be okay if I leave you now? Will Margaret be home tonight? I don't want you to be alone."

"She's out with her boyfriend, but she'll be back. And Dale, I feel so much better now, just having you here."

She wrapped her arms around him and kissed him long and hard.

"I'd better leave," he said, but he didn't, not right away.

When Lucy was finally alone, she clapped her hands and spun around the room. Things couldn't be more perfect.

She wished her best friend Tyler Anne were right here with her now, so she could tell her everything. But Tyler Anne was in Europe on a Grand Tour she had begged to be released from. Annie's mother knew what was best for her girl, however, so off they went, and they were someplace where Lucy couldn't even call her. Well, of course she could, but she didn't know what hotel in which city in what country. Margaret, when she returned, was not likely to be interested in or approving of the evening's turn of events.

Lucia Rose was feeling rather proud of herself, however, having disposed of both Susan and Gregory. Now, she realized, she had to start thinking about what to do about Roberta.

"Are you still up?" Margaret arrived home after midnight, looking tousled and sleepy. "Did you have a quiet evening?"

Lucy said cautiously, "Well, the strangest thing happened. Greg Reeves came here to see me. I'd never even met him before tonight."

"What did he want?"

"Me, I guess. I mean, he . . . he made advances. Nothing happened. I got rid of him, but I was so scared." She thought of her poor gelding again, remembering the shot that ended its life, and managed to bring forth a few tears.

"You poor thing," Margaret said, aghast at the news. "Are you sure you're okay? You should have called me. Paul's number is on my speed dial. I would have come right home to be with you."

"I called Dale, and he came right over. He's going to kick Greg out of his room at the apartment. So I guess I'm going to have two rooms, his and Susan's. Won't that be nice?"

Margaret wondered at the glee with which Lucy told her of her expanded living quarters, and the rapid disappearance of her tears. What a relief to know that she wouldn't have to devote any concern to little Lucy in the days to come. "I guess everything has worked out to your satisfaction," Margaret said. "I'm going to take a bath and go to bed, and I'll see you in the morning."

Abandoned by Margaret, Lucy turned on the television, and watched a couple of reruns of old, old sitcoms, before she herself went to bed. Tomorrow was moving day, so she'd be up early. José had agreed to bring a van in from Queens to get her things to the Reeves' apartment. Roberta had said that she could bring in her clothes any time after nine, when Carlotta was back from church. Likely Roberta and Dale would be sleeping in, but Lucy had assured her that she had a number of tasks she wanted to complete before the week began, so she would be occupied.

Before she lay down to sleep, Lucy compiled a list, actually two. One was suggested guests for Dale's birthday party, and the other was a listing of women's names. Poppy would have recognized all of them as prominent committee ladies whose names showed up frequently in her "Social Scene" column, and Margaret knew most of them as well. Lucy only knew of them because they were all involved in Roberta's current charity projects as members of various committees or as purchasers of tickets to forthcoming galas.

Just before she turned out the light, she added Lorna Hutchison's name to both lists.

Everything was just too easy.

Chapter 17

To mark the departure of her houseguest, Margaret had finally bought a few croissants for breakfast, at a bakery on her way home from dinner with De Vere.

"Be sure to call me if ever I can be of help," Margaret said. "And by the way, I heard that Carolyn Sue is coming to town in the next couple of days. You'll want to see her, I'm sure. She'll either be staying at her hotel, the Villa d'Este, or at Paul's place. I'll tell her to call you at Roberta's apartment when she gets in."

Lucy sighed. "Sometimes Carolyn Sue is worse than a mother. She has so many rules about the way I'm supposed to behave, the clothes I should wear. You know, she once demanded that I turn blond. Wouldn't I look silly as a blonde? And she's never thought my hair was big enough. She wanted me to grow it longer and puff it out to here with hair spray, like every other female in Texas. She doesn't take no very well, does she? And she hated the fact that I worked really hard to lose my Texas accent after they made fun of me in Boston. And I don't use all those quaint phrases the good ol' gals use."

"I'm sure Carolyn Sue is just worried about your welfare, and your success in life. She told me herself she feels a great responsibility for you since your mother died."

"I always thought that she was hoping to shed that mean old cuss, Ben Hoopes, and marry Daddy after Mother was killed. But Ben has piles more money than we do, so she must have decided he wasn't worth pursuing. Isn't it funny the way people simply cast off spouses and take up with someone else, as though there was never any good reason to get married in the first place, and there's no really good reason to get married again?"

"Funny, yes, but I do think there are lots of people who marry because they really love the other person, and that feeling doesn't go away."

"I don't think Roberta and Dale stay together because of love," Lucy said. "They never spend much time with each other. She's always so busy. He told me they used to travel a lot and do things together, but not anymore. I'm sure she stays married to him because he's well known and he knows all kinds of cool people. He really deserves something better."

"And who are you thinking would be 'better'?"

"Maybe this Lorna that he's been seeing for ever so long, or at least that's what people say. Or . . . or there might be another who really appreciated him."

"I don't think Roberta would give him up easily," Margaret said. "Lorna's been in the picture for a good long time, but she hasn't managed to pry him loose. And Roberta's had her own little flings, you know. Richard Centner, for one. You heard them talking. He never broke up the Reeves' marriage either."

"That was pathetic, wasn't it? The way she tried to get him back." Margaret had to agree.

Lucy made a mental note to add Richard Centner's name to her lists, after they finished their croissants and coffee, and then she glanced at the Sunday *New York Times*.

"Almost time for José to show up. The building manager was thrilled to give him a couple of hours to help me. Of course, the money did the trick," Lucy said. "Want to come along with us?"

"I think not. I'm planning to lunch or brunch or whatever with a friend I haven't seen for a while."

Then José was knocking on the door. He loaded Lucy's luggage onto a two-wheeler. Margaret and Lucy embraced; although oddly, Lucy had never made such a gesture before. Then she was gone. At last.

Margaret rang Dianne Stark, to confirm their lunch plans.

"Can't wait to see you," Dianne said. "Los Angeles is as strange and wonderful as ever, but I was taken to dinner at a wonderful place called Vincenti's. It's run by the wife of that friend of yours who died, Mauro. Lots to report."

"As do I," Margaret said.

"You sound ominous. I hope you haven't stumbled over another dead person."

Margaret laughed. "Heavens, no. I've sort of run out of murder victims, which pleases De Vere no end."

They decided to splurge and enjoy the Sunday buffet at the Waldorf, which provided massive amounts of food in all possible varieties.

"I'll meet you near the clock in the lobby," Margaret said, "for the one-thirty seating. I wish I hadn't eaten two croissants for breakfast."

At twenty after one, Margaret presented herself in the soaring lobby of the Waldorf. The center had been filled with tables loaded with a hundred dishes: huge roasts of beef; platters of thin, rosy salmon; great tubs of whipped cream cheese; pots of caviar; trays of sliced cold meats; warming trays of sausage, bacon, and eggs; a variety of pastas; wicker baskets of steamed oriental dumplings and tiny eggrolls; vats of chicken variously prepared; an array of cheeses of the world; piles of fresh fruit; and a long table loaded down with cakes and all manner of pastries.

"Think we'll get enough to eat?" Dianne asked when she appeared five minutes later, and they were shown to their table. Dianne was wearing a pale-green silk suit, and Margaret knew that not a single drop of tasty pasta sauce, no fragment of salami, no tiny dollop of whipped cream would sully the front of the jacket during the meal. Dianne had a special gift for neatness.

So they filled their plates and brought them back to the corner of Peacock Alley where they'd been seated. Dianne recounted her adventures in Los Angeles, and Margaret reported on the arrival and departure of Lucia Rose, and all the high points in between.

"I know Dale and Roberta, of course," Dianne said. "Is he pulling a midlife crisis sort of thing on the poor girl? Will she be able to defend her virtue, or more to the point, defend herself against the wrath of Roberta Reeves?"

"I think little Lucy is more than adequately equipped to take care of herself," Margaret said. "I'm just afraid she may step into quicksand because she's so sure of herself. I don't believe that thing with Greg Reeves, and I am ashamed to confess that I think she had something to do with causing the rift between Susan and her mother. All with an eye for attaining resident status in the apartment. I can't imagine what she'll get herself up to now. Who's next?"

Margaret and Dianne locked eyes, and Dianne smiled. "Are you thinking Roberta?" Margaret asked. "What could Lucy do to her? I mean, Roberta is pretty well able to take of herself, too."

"I have never underestimated the determination of young women," Dianne said. "Of course, I had the perfect example in my own sister. Let's hope Carolyn Sue arrives in the nick of time and sets Lucy straight. But, after all, she hasn't done anything too terrible."

"Not yet," Margaret said. "Let's say we try some of that cake with the gold leaf on top while I tell you about little Lucy's unilateral plans for Dale's birthday party."

Little Lucy, meanwhile, had directed a besotted José where to deposit her several pieces of luggage in the cheerful big bedroom that was all hers. They worked quietly, because Carlotta had informed them that Madame and the doctor had not yet awakened, but Mrs. Frost provided them with coffee from the batch she had prepared for the master and mistress of the household.

"They sleep until noon on Sunday," Carlotta said.

"But Dr. Reeves told me he was playing golf today," Lucy said. "Maybe I should wake him to remind him."

Carlotta didn't think that was a good idea. In fact, she didn't seem pleased at all to be welcoming Lucy to the apartment. She and José muttered to each other in Spanish, and Lucy heard the word *puta*. Lucy said, "I speak the language, you know. Most of my friends back home were Latinos, so please do not refer to me as a woman of loose morals, Carlotta, or you may find yourself looking elsewhere for work."

"Excuse me, miss," Carlotta said.

José said, "Señorita Lucy, I must return the van to my friend in Queens, and I fear to get a parking ticket on the street where I left it." They had stopped on the side street and brought Lucy's luggage in through the side entrance, under the maroon canopy.

"I have everything," Lucy said. "Thank you so much for helping me." She pressed some bills into his hand. "Show José out, Carlotta. I'll just hang up my clothes. And I do think you should awaken the doctor and remind him of his golf game. Please do it now." She turned her back on them and opened the first suitcase.

Carlotta shrugged. She knew if she awakened Mrs. Reeves, she would have to endure some angry words, but perhaps the girl was right. The doctor did go golfing a lot, and he would be angry if he missed an appointment to play, but if she reminded him, he was likely to be grateful. A dilemma, to be sure, but if there was too much anger, she would start feeling unwell, and would hide herself in her room until it blew over.

Lucy kept to her room, listening for Dale. Finally she heard him speaking to Carlotta. "Never mind what Madame says, Carlotta. I'm glad you woke me. I've missed my tee time, but I can still get to the course in time for a round. I'll hook up with some group other than the one I usually play with. You're so clever to remember my game."

Carlotta said something that Lucy couldn't hear.

"She did? Lucy told you to wake me? Isn't she the clever one to remember."

"Too clever by half." Roberta had joined them. "Is she here already? Good. I have some things she must do at once." Then she knocked on Lucy's door. "I need you as soon as you're able," Roberta said.

Lucy opened the door a crack, and Dale waved to her from behind Roberta's back. "I'll only be a minute, Roberta," Lucy said. "Just hanging up my clothes. I'll meet you in your office." She waited until she was sure Dale had departed. She didn't really want to talk to him this morning with Roberta around, but she wondered if he'd told his wife her story about Greg. If he had, she would certainly bring it up, and she'd better remember the details she'd told Dale.

But Roberta didn't mention Greg when they met in the drawing room, which had become considerably less cluttered since Lucy had been handling things.

"I want you to call Terry Thompson right away, and tell her that the Stacy Gallery is buying a full page in the program for the hospital benefit. The hospital saved Barbara Stacy's child's life, and she wants to show her appreciation. Although," she added grimly, "sometimes I wonder if a child is worth it. Well, go on. I know it's Sunday, but Terry never sleeps and she doesn't go out on Sundays. She needs to know as soon as possible because Stacy wants the inside back cover, and I don't want Terry to give it to someone else."

Before Roberta went off to arrange her hair and face, which had not been carefully managed due to being awakened suddenly, she said crossly, "You'd think Dale would stay home one Sunday at least, instead of always trundling around a golf course with a bunch of boring buddies."

"He needs his relaxation, I'm sure," Lucy said. "He works hard all week."

"Listen, miss. I don't need you to tell me what my husband needs." Roberta stamped out of the room, and Lucy looked up Terry Thompson's phone number in the Rolodex, thinking it would be a good idea if Roberta invested in a computer. She could keep all the names and addresses in a database, and organization would be much more streamlined.

Sure enough, Terry Thompson was at home this Sunday morning.

"Mrs. Thompson, it's Lucy Grant, Roberta Reeves' assistant. Sorry to trouble you, but Mrs. Reeves asked me to tell you . . ." Lucy hesitated. "To tell you that you needn't save the inside back cover of the program for anyone special."

"That's good. I half promised it to . . . to someone or other."

"But the Stacy Gallery is going to buy a page, and you should call Barbara Stacy about it. I have that number right here." Lucy smiled to herself. A little mischief is better than none. "I think I got it all right. Mrs. Reeves was upset this morning, and wasn't quite clear about the program."

"Just between you and me, dear, when Roberta gets in a tizzy about something, she's not clear about anything."

"Oh, Mrs. Thompson, Mrs. Reeves is giving a surprise birthday party for Dr. Reeves on the twenty-third. She hopes you'll come. I'll be sending an invitation, but I thought as long as I had you on the line . . ."

"Love to," Terry Thompson said. "But what do you give a celebrity dentist for his birthday?"

"I'm sure gifts are not expected," Lucy said.

Then she called Lorna Hutchison, who fortunately

was not in, or not answering her phone, and left a message on her answering machine, inviting her to Dale Reeves' surprise party. "If you want to send regrets, please call me, Lucy Grant, rather than Mrs. Reeves, since I'm keeping track of the guest list."

More mischief is even better.

Chapter 18

*M*argaret *left* the Waldorf feeling that she would never be able to eat again. Her apartment felt strangely empty with Lucy gone, but she looked forward to not having someone going and coming, usually late at night. At least she'd be able to return her clothes to the closet. In any case, she expected she'd see Lucy again when Carolyn Sue rolled in, and when she did, she'd ask for her apartment key. She didn't want Lucy showing up unexpectedly after a tiff with Roberta or Susan, Greg or Dale. Or even with the drug-dealing Frankie. Then she decided she had best set her own life in order. Dianne was so enthusiastic about her upcoming training to be a caregiver that Margaret had been put to shame.

No, she wouldn't study veterinary medicine, nor would she teach riding to adolescents, as Giovanni had suggested. But she would turn down all invitations to serve on committees, and since she didn't plan to eat again for the rest of her life, she would also turn down invitations to lunch and to parties of all sorts. Except perhaps Dale Reeves' birthday party. She was curious to see how that event unfolded.

Poppy rang her late in the afternoon as she dozed over *The New York Times.* "I don't know if you continue to be interested in the activities of your young Texas friend," Poppy said.

"Do you have something to tell me? She's moved out and gone to live with Roberta and Dale."

"Has she indeed? Well, my dear, I had an astonishing phone call from Lorna. It seems she was invited to a birthday party for Dale. Apparently Roberta issued the invitation, of all things, but the bearer of the news was none other than your Lucia Rose. What do you suppose that's all about? I doubt that Roberta would have the woman in her home."

"Maybe little Lucy has taken it upon herself to . . ." She almost said, To cause trouble, but instead said, "To add a little fun to the event. Maybe she unwisely thought it would please Dale. I did tell her about Lorna and Dale. Maybe she'll decide to invite Richard Centner as well." Margaret was now determined not to miss this party. There was clearly no telling what Lucy would come up with.

"Not only that about Lorna," Poppy said, "but finally the tales of Dale squiring the young miss around town have gotten about. Everybody's talking about it. Audrey Cheever says she always knew the girl had been brought in by Roberta to distract Dale from Lorna."

"So she indicated to me. And if Audrey has the news, soon everyone will. It may be that Lucy's life is going to get very complicated."

Margaret was unable to concentrate further on deciding what she should do with her life, although the idea of selling bijoux at some fashionable Fifth Avenue shop held a certain appeal. She certainly knew a bit about good jewelry, both real and the costume variety, and Bedros had always told her that she was good with

the public. Even Giovanni praised her way with difficult
and rich women. Perhaps she should inquire about sales
positions at Landau in Trump Tower, the Kenneth J.
Lane shop, or Erwin Pearl, who had a delightful line and
even elegant British-accented saleswomen. She didn't
think she was quite ready to approach Tiffany's, Bulgari,
Cartier, or Harry Winston. She'd have to do some home-
work to be prepared to sell multicarat diamonds.

She idled away the rest of the day, feeling just a bit
lonely. Well, Carolyn Sue would be in tomorrow or the
next day, and that always meant a blur of shopping.
Surely there were plenty of fine stores in Dallas, but Carolyn Sue just loved New York shops. There would be get-
togethers with De Vere and Paul, tea at the Villa d'Este,
perhaps even a quick tour of Carolyn Sue's latest real
estate acquisitions. She loved showing off her buildings,
as though she lived in the middle of a life-sized Mo-
nopoly game.

Just to feel that she was doing something about
her employment situation, Margaret scanned the Help
Wanted section of the *Times,* but without much hope
that the perfect job would spring from the pages. A secretary she wasn't, nor a physician's assistant. Not a short-
order cook, or even a deli-counter woman. It made her
feel useless to be so lacking in marketable skills.

"Look, Roberta, I work very hard for the money that
pays for all this, and I don't see why I can't play golf
once in a while." Roberta had expressed her displeasure
when Dale returned from his round of golf, crowning the
argument with a mighty slam of the door to the bedroom, where she locked herself in, and declined further
discussion.

"I didn't mean to eavesdrop, Dale," Lucy said.

"Pretty hard to avoid," he said. "Don't worry, it's her usual response to my outings. What do you say to a glass of iced tea or lemonade or something, in the living room. I'm sure Mrs. Frost can fix us up with something tasty."

"Why, that would be lovely. And you can tell me how your game went, although you'll find me very stupid about golf. Daddy hates the game, so he never played after the first few times. I think it's because he wasn't very good at it, and he really likes games where he wins.

"If he can't come out ahead in something, he really prefers to hang out with his politician cronies, or go out to the ranch and ride. That's something he does well. I don't think he ever forgave my mother for dying while riding. I've never really forgiven her for getting killed that way." Lucy donned the appearance of deep grief.

"Come on, sit down and tell me all about it. That's the way life is sometimes. You think you've got it all, and something comes along to kill the joy. I've been there. Just that thing with Greg and you last night pretty much did me in. I don't understand the boy."

"Please, let's not talk about it," Lucy said, for she could barely remember the details of the story she'd told him. "I'm sure I'm going to be running into Greg here, and I don't want to cause any more problems. Have you told him yet that he has to move out of his room? Susan's room isn't as big as I thought, so I'm going to need a lot more space."

"It's being taken care of," Dale promised. "Ah, here's Mrs. Frost with our drinks."

Lucy feigned not to notice Mrs. Frost's disapproving glance at the two of them seated cozily together on a sofa. But if Dale didn't care, why should Lucy?

"Thank you so much, Mrs. Frost," Lucy said. "That will be all."

Mrs. Frost frowned briefly at Lucy's assumption of the tone of the lady of the house. "Will Mrs. Reeves be wanting anything, Doctor?" She decided to ignore Lucy.

But Lucy was not to be ignored. "You might knock on the door and ask. She was a bit upset earlier."

"I shouldn't wonder," Mrs. Frost said, and left them together.

"She seems a little impertinent for a servant," Lucy said.

"Mrs. Frost has been with us for a long time," Dale said, "and she practically brought Susan up along with nannies, because Roberta was always so busy. She probably feels like a member of the family. She was very disappointed when Roberta told Susan she had to move her things out. We allow her to be outspoken because she sometimes tells us hard truths we'd otherwise miss."

They heard the chime of the doorbell, and after a moment, Carlotta appeared. "It's Mr. Greg," she said. "I asked him why he didn't just come in instead of making me run from my room to answer the door, but he said you'd know. He won't come in here until I've announced him."

"Did you speak to him about last night?" Lucy asked nervously. "I didn't mean to cause him trouble. . . ."

"But he didn't mind causing you trouble. Yes, I've spoken with him, and told him I wanted him out of this place immediately. I said that I didn't need to explain why."

"And I'll bet he said you did have to explain."

"How did you know?"

"Because he probably didn't think he'd done anything

wrong. Who am I to him? Just some kid who's in New York looking for a good time."

"I don't know what you are," Greg Reeves said from the door, "but I'm beginning to get an idea. Look, Dad, could I speak to you privately?"

"I'll be in my room, Dale," Lucy said, "if you want to talk later." Before she left, she whispered, "It'll be okay."

But she heard Greg say behind her back, "Where did you dig up that piece of trouble anyhow?" Then she didn't hear anything more.

Lucy listened at her door from time to time, never hearing any sound from the big apartment outside her room. She was growing hungrier by the minute, but she didn't want to risk running into Greg or even Roberta. Finally she unearthed a Power Bar in her handbag, having grown accustomed to carrying some with her, particularly when she went riding alone back home. It comforted her to know that even if she got lost on the prairie, she'd have something to eat. She never dreamed she'd get lost on Park Avenue in New York City.

Finally, quite late, after night had fallen, she heard a faint tap on her door. She opened it a crack and found Dale with something wrapped in a white napkin in his hand. "You didn't join us for dinner, and I thought you might be hungry," he said. "Mrs. Frost managed a sandwich for you."

"Thanks. Want to come in?"

"I think I'd better not. It hasn't been a pleasant day, and I don't want to risk more unpleasantness if Roberta should turn up. I'll be leaving for the office early in the morning, but I expect I'll turn up here around lunchtime. Roberta has said she'll be going out. You and I will go someplace quiet for a bite to eat."

"You can find me in the office, I have a ton of things to do. Did you have trouble with Greg?"

"He wasn't very pleased about the whole business, and of course he denied laying a hand on you. He said you were making it all up. You weren't, were you?"

Lucy opened her eyes wide. "Why would I make up such a story?"

"Greg wondered that, too. He'll have his stuff out of his room by tomorrow night. Then you can settle in."

"Would it be too pushy of me to invite my best girl-friend, Tyler Anne, to stay the night sometime when she gets back from Europe? I mean, I don't want to treat this place like my very own home . . ."

"It is your home," Dale said. "Enjoy the sandwich, and sleep well."

"I do believe I'll dream of you," she said. "The man who saved me from starvation."

He touched her cheek with one hand as he handed her the sandwich with the other. "You were right, things did work out. Good night, sweetheart."

It got easier all the time.

Chapter 19

Roberta was distant and cold as she gave Lucy a list of tasks that absolutely had to be accomplished that morning. "I'll be out most of the day, but if Mrs. Cheever calls around noon, tell her I'm on my way to meet her, although I might be a bit late for lunch, since I'm coming from a fitting, and I have to pick up some shoes. Well, the shoe place is practically across the street from the restaurant, so you can tell her to look for me there; she knows the place. Or not, as she chooses."

Lucy had another proof to check, this one for another benefit. She altered one or two names that were spelled correctly so they looked at first glance like mild obscenities. She initialed the proof with "RR," precisely imitating Roberta's handwriting, with the thick pen she invariably used. No one would ever be able to tell that Roberta hadn't written it, and wouldn't her precious committee ladies be shocked when they saw the printed invitation.

She finished her other chores, and then concentrated on the preparations for Dale's party. Roberta hadn't exactly said yes, go ahead with the plans, but she had as good as okayed it. Lucy had discussed with Mrs. Frost about where to get the cake, but today Mrs. Frost was, well, frosty. Fat, mean, old bitch was Lucy's assessment. Hadn't she been the one to talk about Susan wanting the Georgian tea service? A person had to accept the consequences of her words and her actions.

Dale didn't come home at lunchtime, but Mrs. Cheever did call to find out where Roberta was. "She said to say she might be late. She had a fitting," Lucy said, "and then she was buying shoes. At Bloomingdale's, I think."

"You must be the little girl Roberta hired to help her out. I understand you're doing a fine job."

Lucy held her tongue. She hated to be called a little girl.

"I wonder why you're telling me a lie," Audrey Cheever said.

"But I'm not," Lucy said, wondering what lie she was talking about.

"Roberta Reeves swore months ago never again to set foot in Bloomingdale's in this or any other lifetime. Someone treated her badly there, and Roberta doesn't stand for that sort of thing. Never mind, I know where I can find her. You be careful now, young lady. Don't let yourself be used by people who are smarter than you are."

Later, Lucy heard the phone ring elsewhere in the apartment, but Carlotta must have answered it. She was tempted to call Dale's office, but she thought he might not like to be disturbed while he was with a patient. She wanted to hear his voice, though, and the temptation remained strong until Susan Dillon burst into the office.

"You lying little bitch," Susan screamed. "You framed me, and now my mother won't speak to me. And my brother called me to tell me what you accused him of."

Lucy placed some documents carefully in a folder and

then managed to look up at Susan, who appeared red-faced and unkempt. "I don't know what you're talking about. Your brother behaved very badly, so I expect he would deny everything. And your mother asked me to accompany her to your room and witness her discovery of that ugly old silver pitcher hidden under your clothes."

"And how did it get there?" Susan's shrieking voice had subsided a bit, but not much.

"I guess Roberta's assumption was that you stole it and hid it there." Lucy shrugged. "I don't know one way or the other; I just saw it when she found it."

"And it's not ugly, you ignorant Texas bumpkin. It's a beautiful antique piece, worth a lot of money, and it's been in our family for ages." Susan now looked as though she was going to cry. "I'm going to lie down until Mother gets back."

"Don't even think of using the room that used to be yours," Lucy said. "It's my room now."

Susan did not close the door gently.

A few minutes later, Mrs. Frost knocked and entered. "What did you say that so upset Miss Susan? She was tearing around the apartment like a madwoman. I know she did wrong or it looks that way, but I can't believe it of my little pet. She was always such a good child, and she loved those old silver pieces."

"Why, Mrs. Frost," Lucy said, "you yourself said that she was afraid her mother would sell the set and she wanted to inherit it. No wonder she hid that one piece away."

"I said no such thing." Lucy just looked at her, smiling faintly. "And now Miss Susan has telephoned Mr. Gregory, if you can believe that. They hate each other, don't speak unless it's absolutely necessary. She wants him to come here to talk about you and your wicked behavior. I don't like to think what you're up to, miss, interfering and causing everybody trouble. And don't think I don't know about you and the doctor creeping around here and snuggling up together." Mrs. Frost lifted her double chin defiantly. "If it continues, I will have to inform Madame. She will not be pleased."

Lucy thought it would be wise to remove herself from the apartment, so as not to encounter Susan again, or worse, Greg Reeves.

She made a few quick phone calls to some of Roberta's most reliable committee members, doing a respectable imitation of Roberta's voice and telling their answering machines that a major planning meeting had been postponed, giving each a different rescheduled day. Tomorrow she would call them all back as herself, Roberta's entirely capable assistant, to tell them that Mrs. Reeves had made a terrible mistake, and they should attend the meeting on the day originally scheduled. That would put Roberta on the spot, and confirm the widely held belief that she was totally incapable of handling her chores, while Lucy would look the epitome of efficiency.

Then she left and browsed the designer boutiques on Madison Avenue, until it was late afternoon and she felt she could safely return to the apartment. For a moment she regretted the loss of Margaret's companionship. Margaret didn't do a thing with her life and was probably sitting at home reading one of her books. The thought of Margaret's elegant apartment and even the tiny bedroom that had been hers made her feel terribly alone.

As Mrs. Frost had predicted, Madame was not pleased when she stormed in shortly after Lucy's return.

"Why did you tell Audrey Cheever I was at Bloomingdale's? I told you exactly what to say to her, but you had a better idea. So she went off to look for me, and I waited at the restaurant for hours until she finally showed up. It threw my whole schedule off. Sit down, I have something else to say to you." Lucy sat and Roberta stood in front of her. "I will not condone your association with my husband. You're out to make trouble, I know it, and I won't have you enticing Dale into your web."

"Oh, Roberta, where did you get such an idea? Dr. Reeves has never been anything but formal and polite to me, and I think I've been the same to him. He did take me out to lunch when I first arrived, because you were out, and he felt sorry for me, being an outsider and alone in the city. It was never anything more than that."

Of course, Roberta was aware of Audrey's tendency to overdramatize and spread gossip based on flimsy assumptions, so she took a step back.

"All right, as long as you swear that what I've been hearing is untrue. . . ."

"It is untrue. I'm trying hard to do my best for you, Roberta, nothing more. I just try to be pleasant to Dr. Reeves, since he's allowing me to live in his . . . your apartment."

"Now, now, dear. No tears. Why don't you take a break now and join us later for dinner. Dale has invited a nice young associate from his office to meet you. You two might hit it off."

Like I'm dying to meet another dentist, Lucy thought. "That will be lovely, Roberta," she said. "Thank you for not being angry with me."

"Things have been very difficult lately," Roberta

said. "The business with Susan and Greg has really distressed me."

"I hope you're still planning to have the party for Dr. Reeves' birthday."

"Yes, I've even invited a few people. We'll have to go over the details when I have a free moment. There's so much to organize."

Lucy didn't tell her, right then, that all of the organization was nearly complete. The cake had been ordered; the bartender had been hired; she'd arranged to have the barbecue overnighted from one of her favorite places in Dallas; she'd found a party-goods supplier that would provide the fairy lights and decorations, extra chairs and everything else needed, and even a wholesale florist who would bring in pots of chrysanthemums and other fall flowers to decorate the terrace.

"I suppose what I need is a list of guests to invite. I . . . I hope I may invite Lady Margaret. She was so good to me when I first arrived."

"Yes, certainly. And what about your friend Prince Paul Castrocani?" Roberta liked having a few titles at her affairs.

"That would be fun," Lucy said. "And Paul's mother is coming to New York in a few days. If she's still here at party time, perhaps she could be invited."

Although she was no longer Principéssa Castrocani, Carolyn Sue's presence at an event was always a plus for the socially ambitious.

"I'd love to have her," Roberta said. "You arrange that." Roberta had regained something like good humor. "Run along and make yourself pretty for Harvey Bloom. He's a charming boy, single, with a good future. Very interested in culture, always going off to concerts and the theatre. You'll like him."

He sounded perfectly awful to Lucy, but she smiled and ventured to her room. Neither Susan nor Greg was around, but she caught a whiff of something delicious that Mrs. Frost was cooking for dinner. She never seemed to eat regularly since she'd been here, so she was looking forward to dinner, Harvey or not, although she would have preferred an intimate meal with Dale in some cozy restaurant, or even a snack grabbed on the way to a club.

She wondered what Frankie was up to. If he'd been arrested as he was worried he'd be, she hadn't read it in the newspapers, although she'd been pleased to see that Poppy Dill had in fact mentioned her in "Social Scene" the other day. "Beautiful young Dallas socialite Lucia Rose Grant" had sounded real fine to her, even if being a socialite in Dallas was the last thing she wanted to be known for. She had Frankie's cell phone number, and thought that if Harvey Bloom ate his fill and departed early, she might call Frankie and meet him at Tunnel late that night. She didn't think he was as bad as Paul and others made him out to be, and she liked his dark Latino good looks. He was a lot of fun, and she suspected that the drug rumor was simply the same old prejudice against Latinos.

Harvey Bloom turned out to be everything she expected, although far more pompous and self-involved than she imagined he'd be. It was evident that he was immediately taken with her, but Lucy managed to remain some distance from him during the cocktail hour, and she was seated across the table from him at dinner. Harvey, however, directed most of his conversation to her, and now and again she caught Dale's eye and noticed his amused smile when Harvey made yet another fatuous remark.

"I enjoy sports," he said. "Football, basketball, the things men like."

"My father had a box for the Cowboys' games," Lucy said. "I went to the game every Sunday, and of course, the team used to hang out at our house. The coach liked that because Daddy didn't allow any misbehavior that might get them into the papers or jail. Troy Aikman and I liked to talk about how plays were developed. I was so happy when he won three Super Bowls, because he was a real cute kid, not all that smart, but football players don't have to be intellectual giants. I guess the same is true of the spectators."

Dale had the decency to cover his laughter with a napkin, but Harvey looked at her in awe. "You really know Troy Aikman?"

"Like a brother," Lucy said sweetly.

After that, Harvey could barely bring himself to speak to her, gazing upon her as if she had suddenly become the sun and the moon. It only confirmed her belief that the combination of men and sports resulted in complete idiocy. She'd found the Dallas quarterback quite entertaining, and she was aware of his records and status in the game, but as far as she was concerned, he was never going to rid the world of poverty and injustice, or find a cure for cancer.

Then she couldn't resist saying, "I know everybody on the team, and everybody on the Mavericks and the Stars as well. Daddy is a big sports fan." How soon would Harvey leave, and then how soon could she leave?

"Miss . . . um . . . Grant, my appointments start early

tomorrow, so I guess I'd better go home," Harvey said, to Lucy's great joy. "I have to drive to New Jersey. I just bought a real nice house there. I'd like to have you come for a visit sometime."

"Perhaps I'll have a chance to do that," Lucy said, but thought, Not in this lifetime.

"Thank you for inviting me to dinner, Mrs. Reeves," Harvey said. "I've had a wonderful time. Miss . . . um . . . Grant . . ."

"Just call her Lucy," Dale said. "Everybody does, probably even the Dallas quarterback." He winked at Lucy behind Harvey's and Roberta's backs.

"I think Troy used to call me Sweetie Pie," Lucy said sharply, "but Lucy is fine." She suspected that Harvey was getting up the nerve to ask her out, to ask for an autograph from the hand that had probably touched Troy Aikman. Sorry, I don't give autographs, she thought to herself, unless you're willing to pay big bucks or at least get out of my life.

"Lucy," Harvey managed to say, "I'd like to call you sometime. Maybe we could go to a concert or something?"

"I look forward to your call," Lucy said, planning to be very busy indeed for at least the next three months.

Harvey departed, looking like a man who had just won the lottery. Lucy said, "If you don't mind, Roberta, I'm going out to meet some friends. I won't be too late."

"You should have had Harvey drive you. I know he'd have loved to."

"Roberta, Lucy doesn't want to be fixed up with Harvey Bloom. Surely you can see that. Let her go and have some fun," Dale said, then turned to Lucy. "Harvey is an excellent dentist, but not your type, I think."

"Bull's-eye on that one," Lucy said.

"You'll be careful being out late at night, won't you?" Dale said. "We're responsible for your welfare now that you're living here."

"I'll be perfectly all right," she said. "They're people just as nice as Harvey."

She reached Frankie's cell phone, and he promised to meet her at the club. "Great crowd here tonight. Leo and them, and somebody said Puffy was going to show up." She could hear the crowd noises in the background.

"Half an hour maybe. See you then."

Chapter 20

*W*ell, Puffy Combs didn't show, nor did Leonardo Di-Caprio, but Lucy and Frankie had a fine old time dancing and talking, and she didn't pay much attention when he went off into the corner to talk with nervous men and cool, confident women who wanted to score a little extra joy. Frankie had tried often enough to get her to sample his wares, but Lucy hated to feel out of control even momentarily, and she knew she had to keep her wits about her.

She did have a couple of drinks, but she wasn't the slightest bit tipsy when she got back to the apartment. It was dark and quiet, with only a dim light on in the hallway that led to her room. She was feeling quite pleased with herself. Not only had she messed up Roberta's relationship with her daughter, blackened Greg's reputation, and slightly damaged Roberta's credibility as a chairperson, but she was sure that Dale was in the throes of a serious infatuation that she could work to her advantage. She knew she couldn't remain at the Reeves' apartment for long, but she had high hopes that Carolyn Sue's appearance in the city would lead to satisfactory domestic arrangements.

"Is that you, Lucy?"

She jumped at the sound of Dale's voice.

"I couldn't sleep until you got home; I was that worried about you." He moved out of the shadows and took her in his arms. "I'm so glad to see you back safe and sound."

She didn't resist the impulse to place her head on his shoulder. "Nothing to worry about," she murmured, "but I'm glad to be back right here with you. I'd better go to bed now, though, but I'll see you in the morning."

"You will, sweetheart," he said, and kissed her. Neither of them noticed Roberta standing in the doorway of her bedroom. "Sleep well, Lucy."

Lucy knew he was watching her walk down the long hallway, but she was thankful he didn't try to follow. All that stuff could come later, when her path was clear of obstacles, like Roberta.

Because of her several drinks at the club, Lucy didn't sleep well, and woke feeling unwell. In the morning, she lay in bed drowsing, too tired to get up. When she finally did get up, Dale had departed and Roberta was in her office, talking to someone on the phone. She's always angry, Lucy thought as she sat herself down to work. She hoped Roberta would leave soon so she could call back the ladies and change the planning meeting back to the original day.

"Good morning," Lucy said cheerfully when Roberta was finished with her call.

Roberta just looked at her thoughtfully, then said, "I had occasion to speak with Terry Thompson this morning. She told me something interesting."

Lucy waited expectantly, with just a little knot of nervousness in her already unsettled stomach.

"It's about the Stacy Gallery ad in the hospital benefit

program. Or perhaps I should say, the ad that would have been. Barbara Stacy has canceled completely because she can't have the back inside cover. And Terry tells me that you instructed her to give it to someone else."

"There's been a mistake, then," Lucy said. "I told her no such thing."

Roberta shrugged. "Have it your way, but Terry is a careful and responsible person. And she knows what she heard, all the more clearly because when she called Barbara to confirm a page inside the book, Barbara explained her preference firmly, along with the agreement she and I had made about the cover. Have the proofs gone back to the printer? Good. Have you called to remind the committee people about the planning meeting?" Lucy nodded. "Now, about Dale's birthday party . . ."

Lucy handed her a detailed list of everything that had been arranged, leaving only the guest list to be settled. "I thought you'd prefer to call people. It would be presumptuous of me to invite people to your husband's party."

"Suddenly you are worried about being presumptuous? I find that hard to believe, given what I've heard from Mrs. Frost and Carlotta, and what I've seen with my own eyes."

"Roberta, I've done nothing wrong. Those mean old gossips are afraid they'll have more work to do, so they want to get rid of me. They're the ones who are telling you lies."

"You understand lies pretty well, don't you? Well, just as Terry knows what she hears, I know what I see. Keep away from my husband. I mean it."

Lucy wondered if she ought to warn Dale that his wife

had been spying on them. But she'd just deny it, and say she inadvertently saw something she shouldn't have. Lucy didn't want to scare him off, just when things were going so well.

Roberta had calmed down by the time they sat down to compose a guest list for the birthday party. Margaret was included, and her escort; Paul and his mother; many people whose names Lucy recognized from Roberta's committee rosters—Dianne Stark, Terry Thompson, Audrey Cheever, and others; Susan and Greg and spouses were on the list, although Roberta expressed doubts that they would appear; Harvey Bloom, alas, was also invited, but Lucy figured she could stick close to Paul; and finally she saw the name of Richard Centner.

"Rich and I haven't been close for ages, but it was so nice seeing him the other day that I wanted to invite him. It will certainly add to the surprise for Dale if he's here." Lucy thought that an appearance by Lorna Hutchison would probably be sufficient surprise—for both of them.

"Since Mr. Centner works for Carolyn Sue now," Lucy said, "it's perfectly reasonable to invite him if she's invited."

"You take care of Margaret and Paul and Carolyn Sue, and I'll call the others," Roberta said.

"We'll have to think of a way to keep Dr. Reeves away from the apartment until everybody is here," Lucy said.

"I'm sure you'll manage to think of something," Roberta said. "You're good at thinking up little plots. In fact, I'll leave that all to you."

The next item up was the arrival of Carolyn Sue. She telephoned Lucy from her suite at the Villa d'Este, and demanded that she pay court at six o'clock on the dot.

"Paul's comin' around at seven-thirty, but I want a good ol' girl-to-girl talk with you first, you hear?"

"Yes, ma'am," Lucy said, and wondered how much Carolyn Sue knew about her recent adventures in New York. Margaret had probably blabbed something, but she knew only that Lucy had stayed out late at the clubs a couple of nights. Big deal. Well, she knew a bit about Dale taking her around, and probably blabbed about that to Carolyn Sue. Another big nothing. Unless Carolyn Sue reported everything back to her father. If that happened, Big Ed would probably hightail it here to New York and drag her back to Dallas and his loving care. At least nobody knew about Frankie.

"I'm seeing Carolyn Sue tonight," Lucy said to Roberta, sorry that she wouldn't have a chance to see Dale today at all. She thought he might at least have called her. "She'll send me home early."

"You give her my best regards, and tell her I'm looking forward to seeing her at the party. Won't take a refusal from her."

"I'll be sure she accepts." The more she thought about Dale's party, the less enthusiastic she was. It was going to be like one of those mystery stories where they bring all the suspects together at the end to solve the crime.

Lucy made sure she looked demure and innocent when she set off to see Carolyn Sue at the Villa d'Este. The cozy, elegant little hotel reeked of the kind of money that Paul's mother was known for. The concierge even offered to accompany her to Mrs. Hoopes' suite, so impressed was the staff that the owner was actually in residence.

"I think I can manage to push a button in an elevator

and get off at the right floor," Lucy said, and took the opportunity when she was alone in the plush elevator and rising silently to the top floor to think herself into being little Lucia Rose Grant, Big Ed Grant's baby girl.

Carolyn Sue herself let her into a remarkably white room, not unlike the glaringly white living room in her Dallas house that Margaret remembered and Lucy knew well.

"Let me look at you! Don't you look precious!" Carolyn Sue hugged her mightily, and nearly damaged Lucy's cheek with the sharp pressure from one of her enormous bejeweled earrings. "Why, you don't look as though New York has damaged you any. To hear Margaret tell it, you're runnin' wild, doin' all kinds of wicked things."

"I'm sure Margaret said nothing of the kind," Lucy said.

"Well, I might be exaggeratin' just a touch, honey, but I got to thinkin' over what Margaret actually did say, and I thought you could use some carin' for by somebody who's known you since you were about as high as one o' them little fence posts out at the ranch."

"Carolyn Sue, I'm bigger than a fence post now, and smarter. I'm doing real well as Roberta's assistant, and I've made a few friends here," Lucy said, hoping Carolyn Sue wouldn't ask to meet them. She didn't think Frankie would quite cut it, although Harvey Bloom would certainly be approved of in an instant, with some reservations. He wasn't especially stylish or handsome, two things that counted with Carolyn Sue.

Still, Lucy understood that Carolyn Sue was extremely grateful for the good dental work she'd received over the years, so she liked dentists as a concept, although not necessarily as beaux for Lucia Rose. She'd certainly agree that they were generally not liked by most people, so would probably demand too much love and attention from a girlfriend or wife.

"Sit yourself down and tell me everything you've been doin' up here," Carolyn Sue commanded. "And don't tell me about the shops. Know every one of 'em from memory. That Roberta Reeves, now, I've known her to be a terror when she's crossed. Any trouble with her?"

"We get along just fine," Lucy said. "She does have a bit of a temper, but I can handle her. I've managed to get her more organized."

"And the handsome doctor?"

"A very nice man," Lucy said shortly. "He's been kind to me. Oh, before I forget, Roberta is having a surprise birthday party for him next Saturday. She wants you to come. Please do, I've planned it to be wonderful."

"You? Isn't that Roberta's job?"

"She didn't even remember when his birthday was. I reminded her, and then I went ahead and planned it all."

"I suppose I could find time, but I get so little time with my sweet boy."

"Paul can come too, and I was thinking that that nice Mr. Centner should be invited. I know he works for you, and I believe he knows Roberta."

"That he does, only too well, if the gossip is true. It's old gossip by now, but still. Well, I do have to confer with Rich, although I was thinkin' of a more businesslike settin'."

"Good. Will you ask him? I did have him show me apartments, but then something happened between Roberta and her daughter, and the daughter's room was free, so I moved in. More convenient."

"No problem. I'll invite Richie. Should be right entertainin' havin' him there. All we need is Dr. Dale's girlfriend."

"Don't worry," Lucy said. "I've already invited her."

Chapter 21

When the pleasantries were over, Carolyn Sue quizzed Lucy in detail about what she had been doing during her short time in New York. Lucy answered the questions with a fair degree of honesty, although she didn't mention her activities regarding Susan and the silver creamer, or the tale she had told Dale about his son's behavior.

"So all you do is sit there and work on Roberta's charity stuff. Doesn't sound like much of a life for a pretty young thing like you."

"Oh, I'm enjoying it."

Carolyn Sue didn't look convinced. "Doesn't sound a bit like you, honey. You were always out there on the barricades, stirrin' people up. Is the doctor behavin' in a seemly fashion toward you?"

"I don't know how you mean that," Lucy said. "He's a lovely gentleman."

"What I mean is, every dentist I've ever known has this need to be loved. They're all lookin' for affection, since they don't get much of it professionally, if you know what I mean."

"I don't think Roberta loves him much. At least not enough to spend any time with him, or to pay attention to his needs. I try to be nice to him, because he . . . well, he deserves it."

"Mmmm. I've heard that before. So you see to his needs, do you?"

"Well, I did find out when his birthday was. No one else remembered it. Sometimes we talk about stuff he's doing."

"Molars, bicuspids, stuff like that? You're not dumb, Lucia Rose. You know perfectly well what all that can lead to. Roberta's not so young anymore, and I'll bet she wouldn't take kindly to seein' her husband swept off his feet by some pretty young thing like you. You listen to me now. You keep your distance if you want to keep your job."

"I could find another job," Lucy said. "Margaret would find me some other needy society lady to assist."

Carolyn Sue laughed. "Honey, if those ladies get a hint of any shady business involving you and another lady's husband, they wouldn't dream of havin' you deliver their newspapers to the back door, let alone set foot in their homes every day."

"Then I could work for one of the interior designers Margaret knows."

"And who do you suppose those designers have as clients? The same ladies. That pack of refined furniture pushers isn't goin' to risk losin' business because the help is a wench with the reputation of husband stealer. I know all these people. You walk the straight and narrow from now on, you hear?"

"Yes, ma'am." Lucy sounded contrite, but Carolyn Sue eyed her suspiciously.

"You look me in the eye, miss, and promise."

She promised. She had no choice, because if she didn't, Big Ed would hear about it and bring her home.

"We don't need to discuss it further," Carolyn Sue said. "Look at the time! My boy's late, as usual. Ah, here he is now."

Paul arrived, looking sleek and handsome. He was accompanied by an attractive man, wearing jeans with a sharp crease, a tweed jacket over a pale-blue dress shirt and no tie, and polished loafers.

Carolyn Sue flung herself at the man and kissed him on the mouth. "Sam, honey. How good to see you!"

The man smiled a crooked smile and disengaged himself from Carolyn Sue's embrace. "Good to see you, too, Carolyn Sue. You're looking better than ever."

"Paul, honey. Thanks for bringin' De Vere around. Lucy, I want you to meet Sam De Vere, Margaret's friend. Sam, this here's Lucia Rose Grant. She was stayin' with Margaret for a time. Margaret took her in, kinda as a favor to me."

"Hello," Lucy said. She looked at him with lowered lashes, and smiled. The look always worked with men. "I've heard a lot about you." Not strictly true, but that always worked, too.

De Vere looked her over. Margaret had told him that Lucy was a beauty, and she certainly was.

"Looking good, Lucy," Paul said. "People were saying they'd seen you at the club with Frankie Martinez the other night. Remember what I told you about him. He's really bad news."

"Why would that be?" Carolyn Sue asked.

"Paul's right. He's not an ideal companion," De Vere said, "as usually is the case when a young man is known to the police."

"Oh, Lucia, are you consortin' with bad types? Haven't you learned your lesson? Why, you went through all that business with the Garcia boy and his sisters. You're lucky you didn't end up in jail for mutilatin' her hair. At least you didn't kill her, like you planned to."

"It's nothing, Mother," Paul said. "Let's drop it."

"If our little Lucy is associatin' with someone known to the police, it's somethin', not nothin'."

"Frankie hasn't done anything wrong, and neither have I," Lucy said. "We just like to dance at the club and have a good time. And just because he made a couple of mistakes when he was a kid, nobody will forget it. It's not fair."

De Vere said, "His 'mistakes,' as you call them, haven't quite stopped, Miss Grant. He's got a thriving business in illegal substances, and one of these days, fairly or unfairly, he'll have to answer for them."

"I guess you're goin' to have to make me another promise," Carolyn Sue said seriously. "About this Frankie."

Lucy sighed. "Okay, I promise I won't see Frankie again. Not on purpose, anyhow. But how can I avoid bumping into him at the club?"

"You'll do your best," Carolyn Sue said. "And now, that's the end of it. What do you say we get somethin' to eat? I'm starvin'. The Villa d'Este just hired a new chef. Now, I know hotel food isn't supposed to be gourmet cookin', but I hear he's tops, and he'll be sure to give us real good stuff. Sam, why don't you call Margaret and have her join us?"

Margaret could join them, so soon the five of them were seated in the hotel's small dining room, fawned over by the staff and treated to the best the kitchen had to offer.

"It pays to own the place where you eat, doesn't it," Carolyn Sue said complacently as the waiter filled their water glasses for the sixth time. Then she said to Margaret in a low voice, "We got to talk when we're alone. I don't like what I'm hearin'. Lucia's like one of those heat-seekin' missiles. She can find trouble with her eyes closed."

"Is it so bad?"

"Not yet, but she has me worried."

"What are you two whispering about?" De Vere asked.

"Just catchin' up on girl talk," Carolyn Sue said. "Margaret, honey, when we finish our dessert, let's you and me have a nice little chat in the bar. I could go for a Baileys Irish Cream. Paul, why don't you and De Vere take Lucy home and then come back here?"

Margaret felt a pang of what—jealousy, concern?—as De Vere and Paul escorted Lucy through the lobby and out into the night.

"She's too damned pretty," Margaret said.

"Don't you worry about De Vere falling prey to that child. He's too smart, and he's got you. It's Dale Reeves that worries me more. He's probably got a lot less sense than Sam, and he's got Roberta to deal with, day in, day out. She's enough to drive any man into the arms of a fresh young thing like Lucy. Besides, Paul knows Lucy as well as anybody. He'll set Sam straight if he gets any ideas about her."

"You're a comfort," Margaret said. "And I am beginning to think that it wasn't a good idea to let her stay at the Reeves' apartment. I can't be sure, but I don't think she's told me the complete truth about everything."

"Well, we'll be seein' for ourselves at this fool party Lucy's planning for Dale."

"Party? Oh yes, she mentioned something."

"For Dale's birthday. You and me and Paul are invited, and probably Sam, if he wants to come. Thing is, she's gone and invited Lorna, and she wants me to ask Rich Centner. Now, won't that be a fine mess?"

"And Roberta has approved?"

"I'm trustin' that she didn't ask Roberta about the invitations, just went ahead and did it. Anyway, can we get the girl to live someplace else other than practically in Dale Reeves' bedroom?"

"She hated being at my apartment; her room was too small and she made me give up most of my closet for her clothes. Centner showed her some places, but she wasn't about to give up the room in the apartment. I guess it's up to you to convince her she'd better leave and then find her a place in one of your buildings, the way we'd originally planned."

"I'll handle it," Carolyn Sue said grimly, and waved to the waiter. "I'll have another of these Baileys."

Paul and De Vere returned in good time, and the four of them chatted for a time, while up on Park Avenue, Lucia Rose stood in front of the Reeves' building, looking up at the terrace that marked their apartment. Should she just go up and see if Dale was around for a bit of comfort, or should she snag a taxi and head for the bright lights of the downtown clubs and Frankie?

She'd made so many promises to Carolyn Sue that she really had no choice, so it was really a matter of going up and straight to her room, or going to one of the clubs where Frankie had been banned and she wouldn't encounter him.

In the end, sleep won out. The apartment was dark. Either the Reeves were out or had gone to bed. Just as well, but she would have liked the comfort of a few close moments in Dale's arms.

"I thought you'd be out late." Dale was sitting in the dark in the living room off the hallway to her room.

He walked toward her, and when he reached her, he stroked her hair. They kissed, but she drew back. "We can't do this here. What if Roberta . . . ?"

"She's sound asleep. I miss you, especially when Roberta goes on a tear about something that didn't go right. People were calling all evening about how she'd somehow upset their plans because of some meeting she'd postponed and then changed back to the original time. It drives me crazy when she goes on and on. Said she didn't know what they were talking about. I must be getting old."

"You're not! You're just the right age. For me."

"If I really thought so . . ." He stopped and looked at her at arm's length. "Run along to bed, sweetheart. I'll see you in the morning."

"Uh, Dale. I was wondering. Since your birthday is on Saturday, do you think that you and I could do something to celebrate? Like go somewhere in the afternoon? Not stay out late. Roberta may want to take you out to dinner, or something."

"I doubt that she even remembers when my birthday is. Sure, we could do that. It will be fun. I'll think of something."

Well, she'd handled the problem of getting Dale out of the house so that the party-goods supplier could set up the terrace in the afternoon according to her precise instructions. She supposed she could trust Mrs. Frost to oversee the process, since she didn't have to cook, except to heat up the barbecue, which would be delivered the day before. The bartender and waiters would arrive at seven, and the guests were due at seven-thirty, so it would all work out.

And what had he meant by "if I really thought so"? She was beginning to think that maybe there was a future for her and Dale. Even if he was a dentist, he wasn't a dentist from the Harvey Bloom school of Dental Dullness. She wondered if they would live here or somewhere else. Well, Roberta wouldn't give up this place easily, and she'd probably demand a big divorce settlement, probably including the apartment.

It would be okay if they lived in a smaller place, maybe on one of the tree-lined East Side streets. She'd seen a lot of nice town houses in her strolls around the neighborhoods of the East Side, and the area was close enough to Dale's office, so he could still walk to work. Aha! Carolyn Sue would be able to help, but even if she disapproved, Lucy was glad she knew Richard Centner. She could prevail upon him to find them a nice place.

If Roberta took all his money in the settlement, she still had her own substantial inheritance from her mother, which she could persuade Dale to use for a roof over their heads. In no time, he'd bounce back financially. Dentists made a lot of money.

They'd never have to go to any of those stupid charity events that Roberta loved so much. In fact, they probably wouldn't be welcome, because Lucy would be blamed for stealing Dale away from one of their own.

She even imagined that if she and Dale were together,

he wouldn't mind if she went out to the clubs from time to time. He probably wouldn't want to come with her, but that was all right. There were plenty of Frankies around to talk to and dance with. Dale was too serious to enjoy that kind of evening. Maybe, though, he'd want her to do some charitable work, and she'd love to help him save the rain forests. He'd like that. After he'd taken care of the divorce settlement, she'd persuade him to take a long vacation. They could visit the Amazon to see the rain forest for themselves.

Lucia Rose went to sleep imagining the two of them on a slow boat, gliding along the Amazon, with the branches of the huge rain forest trees above them while monkeys chattered in their branches and great red and green parrots swooped down over the boat.

Bliss.

Chapter 22

R*oberta was distant* in the next few days, as she telephoned invitations to the birthday party and kept a list of acceptances.

"I've figured out a way to get Dr. Reeves out of the apartment on the afternoon of the day," Lucy said. "Everyone should be here by the time he gets back."

Roberta didn't ask what the plan was.

"I'll be out that afternoon myself," Roberta said. "I'll need to have my hair done for the party. I suppose you can handle everything in your usual competent fashion. You seem to have taken charge of the event already."

"I can handle everything." Lucy was pleased to think that Roberta wouldn't be around to give orders that might go counter to what she'd planned.

For the next few days, she drilled Mrs. Frost and Carlotta on what was to be done on the terrace, where the lights were to be placed, and the plants. She had Mrs. Frost clear space in the refrigerator to store the barbecue, and went over the menu with her. The wine and other potables were delivered during the week and stored. The bartender would set up the bar himself. Lucy checked the weather forecast a hundred times, but there was no hint of rain. In fact, it would be unseasonably warm for September.

"I suppose Carlotta and I ought to buy Dr. Reeves a present," Mrs. Frost said, "although I can't imagine there's a thing he needs or wants."

"I don't think you need to buy him anything. But you might make a small donation to Save the Rainforest. I know he'd like that."

"Well, that's one worry gone," Mrs. Frost said. "You know, Madame doesn't have many parties here, and you'd think she would, with the number of friends she has. She only ever has a few people to dinner. I like a big party once in a while." Mrs. Frost seemed to have forgotten her early crossness with Lucy.

"The cake will be delivered on Saturday afternoon," Lucy said. "Just keep it hidden, and you can wheel it in on the tea cart that night." She made a note to buy extra candles, in case the bakery didn't include them. She didn't think she should put fifty candles on the cake, but she wanted a lot of them so there would be a blaze of light when the cake made its appearance.

"It's very nice what you're doing for the doctor," Mrs. Frost said, "but . . . but I hope you understand that there are lines you mustn't cross. I'm still a bit puzzled about what you did to Susan and Mr. Greg, but I suppose you have your reasons. Are they coming to the party?"

"They were invited, but I don't know if they accepted. It would be too bad if they were stubborn and refused to come. I wish I could be here to help you set up, but the only way I could think of to get Dr. Reeves out of the house was to make him take me somewhere."

"He could have gone somewhere with his wife."

"She was too busy having her hair done," Lucy said. "I guess that's more important."

"If you say so. Don't you worry. Carlotta and I will take care of everything."

Finally, Lucy had done everything she could to prepare. She had scarcely seen Dale in the preceding days, but he had managed to take her aside one morning, and assure her that he'd made a plan for them on Saturday. "It's going to be a surprise," he said. "I like surprises, don't you?"

"What are you two whispering about?" Roberta said crossly as she came upon them in the living room.

"Nothing," Lucy said smoothly. "Dr. Reeves was explaining that he was going to have his hygienist clean my teeth next week, and he'd give them a checkup."

"Speaking of dentists," Roberta said, "has that nice Harvey Bloom called you? I think you two would make a lovely couple."

"I've spoken to him," Lucy said. She knew she'd be seeing him at the party, so she'd turned down his invitation to dinner and a concert. No way was she going to go off alone with him. "I expect I'll be seeing him soon."

That seemed to please Roberta, although Dale frowned.

"Roberta, could I have you look at some papers in your office?" Lucy asked.

"What's the problem now?"

"No problem. Just something we have to go over."

Roberta was a long time joining her, and when she did finally come to the office, she said, "Dale really doesn't suspect a thing about his party, does he?"

"He hasn't said anything to me," Lucy said, "so I guess he doesn't know anything."

"What is it you want to see me about?"

"I just wanted to tell you that everything is taken care of. Mrs. Frost is actually quite excited about the party. She'd like it if you entertained more."

"I'm not doing any entertaining," Roberta said. "This is all yours, but I hope I'm going to get some credit for it."

"Of course! Dale will think it was all your idea."

Roberta laughed. "I doubt that very much. Well, I do appreciate all your hard work, Lucy."

"It's been fun."

"And how do you plan to get him out of the apartment tomorrow?"

"Oh, he's taking me someplace. A surprise, he said. We'll be back when the guests are here."

Roberta narrowed her eyes. "A surprise indeed."

"Oh, we'll probably just go to the movies. I haven't done that since I've been here."

When Lucy went off, Roberta dialed Audrey Cheever. "You were right, Audrey, she's a conniving little bitch who's got her claws out for my husband, and Dale is just dumb enough to fall for it. As soon as I have time, I'm going for that face-lift. I won't tolerate being displaced by that baggage. I can't be a younger model, but I can look like one for a little while."

She listened, then said, "I know what you've been saying, that I brought her here to entice Dale away from Lorna, but that's simply not true. Besides, Dale hasn't seen Lorna in months, and I doubt he'll ever see her again. But you'll be here tomorrow night, won't you? And you'll do your best to keep Dale occupied, so I can deal with the youngster? She's making me crazy, taking over my life, my apartment, my husband, driving away my daughter and son. No, I shouldn't think either will be here, but I did ask them. Susan is still claiming that the silver creamer was planted in her drawer, and of course she believes that Lucy did it. Why would she? She hadn't even met Susan at the time. Well, yes, she did get to take over Susan's room. And Greg's, for that matter. I mean, she told Dale that Greg had attacked her.

"I guess you're right, Audrey. If she would stoop to fixing matters so I thought Susan was a thief, she could just as easily have made up the story about Greg. He claims she made it up, anyhow. All right, darling, I'll try to stay calm. Be sure to get here early tomorrow. I'm going to need all the support I can get."

Roberta, Dale, and Lucy sat down together for dinner, but no one had much to say. Roberta didn't miss the glances exchanged between her husband and Lucy, but she simply concentrated on her food, and abruptly excused herself as soon as the last crumb of Mrs. Frost's famous carrot cake was finished.

"I need to write some letters," she said. "Good night, Lucy. Come to bed early, Dale. You've been looking tired lately."

"Maybe I'm getting older," he said, but Roberta didn't mention his birthday. Later, from her bedroom, Roberta could hear Dale and Lucy laughing together in the living room. She gritted her teeth. She'd fix the wench once and for all.

Dale did come to bed early, but he had nothing to say to Roberta, who finished the letter she was writing at the little desk in the corner of the room, sealed it, and stamped it.

"What were you and Lucy giggling about?"

"Nothing."

"It was something. You're not a giggler, Dale."

"She was just telling me stories about growing up in Texas, going off to school in Boston, to the horror of everyone in Dallas, who assumed she'd turn communist in a week, fall in love with a black man, and generally come to a bad end."

"Did she?"

"I don't think she's a communist, and she appears to enjoy the company of Spanish-speaking men. I don't know what color they are."

"I mean, is she going to come to a bad end?"

"I imagine Lucy will die as well as she has lived. She's a very pleasant girl, you know. Lively and fun, and she does make me laugh. Good night."

"Good night, Dale. I just want to put my letters out on the hall table so Mrs. Frost can give them to the doorman early in the morning. I want them in the first mail."

When she returned to the bedroom to cream her face and brush her hair, and go all through her pre-bedtime beauty, Dale didn't watch as he usually did. His eyes were closed and he was asleep with a smile on his face.

Roberta soon turned out the light, but she lay awake a long time, thinking about what she had to do.

Chapter 23

"*You seem* out of sorts today," Roberta said when her husband turned up for breakfast the next morning, his birthday. "I know I didn't sleep well myself."

He looked at her, but when she didn't mention his birthday, he poured himself coffee and opened *The New York Times* and settled in behind it.

"Playing golf today?" she said brightly. "It looks like the weather is holding. Pretty soon you won't be able to play in comfort."

"No," he said shortly. "Where's Lucy?"

"I have no idea," Roberta said. "Mrs. Frost said she went out early. She probably has personal business to attend to on the weekend. I don't know why you feel you have to keep track of the girl. It's not as if she's anything to you." Roberta didn't care for the way he looked at her at that moment.

"Possibly she's more to me than you understand," Dale said. "She's thoughtful and amusing." He stood up. "Two qualities which you demonstrably lack."

"Don't be so touchy, Dale," Roberta said. "I know it's your birthday. You always say you don't want people to make a fuss about it. Maybe we could go out to dinner to celebrate it. About seven-thirty? I'll have finished up my little tasks by then. Please?"

"All right," he said. "It might be fun for a change. I'll bring Lucy back by then, and we can go out. Maybe she could come with us."

"Absolutely not. Where are you two going?"

"I haven't decided." He left her then, wandered out to the kitchen, where a startled Mrs. Frost, who never remembered seeing him in her domain, told him that Lucy had gone to see a friend.

"I'll be around when she gets back," he said. "We have an appointment."

Since Lucy still had a key to Margaret's apartment, she let herself in quietly. She could hear Margaret singing off-key in the shower, but a quick check of the apartment told her that there was no one else about. She helped herself to coffee, and waited.

"Ah! You startled me." Margaret emerged from her shower and greeted Lucy without much enthusiasm. "It's a bit early for paying calls, isn't it?"

"I just came to return your key," Lucy said, "and I saw the coffeepot, so . . . I thought you English people always drank tea."

"At teatime certainly," Margaret said. "But I've been in New York so long that I've taken up the habits of the locals. All right, Lucy, what do you want? I know it's something."

"I was kind of wishing that my friend Tyler Anne was around to talk to. Carolyn Sue is nice enough, but she's so bossy. I can't really confide in her. So that leaves you."

"Surely you could talk to Roberta."

Lucy shook her head. "It's Roberta I need advice about."

Margaret waited, half dreading what Lucy might offer. Finally she said, "Really, it's about Dale and me. We've gotten pretty close lately. She doesn't pay any attention to him, but I guess he thinks I do. I mean, I really do. And he likes me a lot. Maybe even loves me. Do you think it's possible?"

"No," Margaret said shortly. "He may be infatuated with a pretty young woman who's been thrust upon his household, but I daresay that's not what I would call love. It's always dangerous to mistake biological urges for the real thing, although they may well lead to it. Just my opinion. Has he mentioned the word? 'Love,' I mean."

"No," Lucy said slowly, "but he does talk about the future and what we'll do together. Doesn't that mean something?"

"No," Margaret said again. "Not a thing. What's Roberta's take on this? Isn't that what you wanted to talk about?"

"She knows something's going on," Lucy said. "But she hasn't said anything, except she's kind of short with me lately."

"I shouldn't wonder," Margaret said. "I know I'd be displeased if I noticed my husband trailing after a potential replacement for me. Lucy, listen. Roberta Reeves is no one to toy with. She's a strong person with a lot of clout in this city. Carolyn Sue said you two have discussed this, and given the nature of the interlocking circles of society, if people here hear what you've been up to, the equivalent people in every city across America are going to know as well. That's just the way things work.

They're probably already gossiping about you in the fitting rooms of Neiman Marcus in Dallas right now."

Lucy looked at her watch. "Too early for that in Dallas. They won't get around to shopping until later. What I'm worried about, Margaret, is what she's going to do. I mean, people get divorced all the time, and life goes on."

Margaret took a deep breath. "Lucia Rose, if you succeed in breaking up this marriage, you'll have to live with the consequences. The first one might be that Dale Reeves will come to his senses, and stay with Roberta. If they do part, he may still come to his senses and avoid marrying you. It's likely that if they divorce, Roberta will take him for everything he's got. His patients could decide they don't want to be treated by a philandering dentist—although that seems unlikely because he's supposed to be so good at his job—but if they do fade away, it may be hard for him to reestablish himself professionally and financially, at least in Manhattan. Finally, Roberta may dig in her heels and refuse to allow a divorce. There are probably ways she could drag things out forever. And where would you be then? Hanging about, waiting for something to happen that isn't going to happen for a very long time, if ever. You would be alone and friendless in a strange city, without a job or the prospect of one. I don't know whether you have money you can draw on, but believe me, this is an expensive place to live."

"I'll have to give him up, you're saying."

"In a manner of speaking."

"I can always go home to Dallas. Daddy will always take me in, even if he is talking about marrying that woman of his."

"So it's home to Dallas and a new stepmummy. Does that appeal to you? I thought not."

"What am I going to do, Margaret?"

"Unless Roberta bows out gracefully, with no hard feelings or high monetary demands, I just don't know. But laying off Dale might be a good idea. Disenchant him, if you can. Listen, Lucy, I understand that this infatuation feels exciting, and all that. But the brave thing to do is to just fade out of his life. And be sure Roberta knows that it has been done. Let the gossip die down. These women don't have long memories for minor scandal. Maybe you can regain Roberta's confidence, find a place of your own where you won't be underfoot in their domestic arrangements, and continue working for her. Or find another job. I told you I had some connections, and both Carolyn Sue and I will help you if we can."

"You're right," Lucy said. "The only thing I want right now is to have a nice party for Dale tonight so he'll remember me and what I did for him. I'll speak to Mr. Centner tonight about an apartment, and maybe in a few days, I'll be gone from there. It will be all right, won't it?"

"Of course," Margaret said, but she wasn't entirely sure about that.

Lucy went back to the Reeves' apartment and double-checked all the party details with Mrs. Frost. Then she laid out the gold-leather Chanel halter-top dress that she would slip into for tonight's party, after she and Dale had returned from their outing. Just in case they got back late and she didn't have time to change immediately, she put on a neat black pantsuit and a cream-colored satin blouse, so that she would look reasonably, if not perfectly, presentable when greeted by a roomful of guests. After the surprise, she'd go off and put on the gold dress, fix up her hair, and repair her makeup.

"Lucy, are you ready?"

Why did she feel so happy at the sound of Dale's voice? No matter what Margaret said, she was certain she was in love with him, and he with her.

"I'm coming!" He was waiting for her near the elevator. "Where are we going?"

"First we're going to have the car take us to Brooklyn to a little outdoor café on the East River that overlooks the bridge and all of Manhattan. It's still warm enough to sit around outside. Then . . . well, maybe I'll wait to tell you."

"Tell me now."

"Then the car will take us up to the Cloisters, and we can look at all the wonderful medieval things they've got there."

She wrinkled her nose. "I hate museums."

"This one is different, trust me. Then, if there's time, we can drive back down to the South Street Seaport, or someplace else. We don't have to decide everything. I did tell Roberta that I'd be back by seven-thirty. She wants to take me out to dinner for my birthday. Just the fact that she remembered it is a gift in itself."

"I have something for you," Lucy said. "I'll give it to you later."

So off they went, like two happy kids on an adventure. Lucy found that the Cloisters wasn't a boring old museum, and she spent a long time gazing at the Unicorn tapestries.

"I wonder if there really are unicorns," she said. "I'll

bet there are a lot of things that we don't see, but they really exist. Margaret told me that her house in England has ghosts and she's seen them, but I don't believe anything I can't see myself."

"Lucy, can you see that I care a great deal for you?"

"I guess so," she said. "I know I care about you."

"What should we do about it?"

"I don't know. I was thinking that I ought to leave the apartment, and you and—"

"Don't leave. Stay with me always."

"I can't. There's Roberta and . . . and everything."

"What if there was no Roberta?"

"I don't understand what you're saying, Dale."

"I'm saying, what if I were to leave Roberta. Then it would be just you and me. We could have a life of our own together."

"Really? You'd get a divorce for me?"

"That's what I'm saying. In fact, I think I'll tell Roberta tonight at dinner. If we're in a public place, she won't dare to make a scene, for fear of who might be there. We'll probably end up at some place where all her friends go, so she won't misbehave in front of all the gossips."

Lucy didn't know whether to believe him or not. "You absolutely promise to tell her tonight?"

"Promise."

It was going to be a party with an extra surprise to it.

Chapter 24

Lucy wished she could go up to the apartment ahead of Dale to be sure everything was in order. She tried to think of some errand she could send him on to delay his appearance. Finally, as they got out of the car just before seven-thirty and it drove away, she said, "Since you're going to be out tonight, I would really love to have some Diet Coke. Mrs. Frost refuses to buy it. I wish I'd remembered it when we were in the car, because the driver could have stopped at a deli, but please, please, would you run over to Madison and get me some?" It sounded pretty weak to her, but Dale was eager to oblige. Then she told the doorman about the surprise party, and asked if he'd delay Dr. Reeves for just a few minutes when he got back.

"I've been sending people up for the last twenty minutes," the doorman said. "But you don't want him seeing the late guests. I got it. I'll take him over to the package room. Some dry cleaning was delivered today, and I'll ask him if it's his. I should be able to keep him for five or ten minutes."

"Great," Lucy said. Another tip was in order, large enough to cover the ten minutes, surely.

She fidgeted in the elevator, frowning at its slowness.

At last she reached the apartment, and found all the guests ready to shout surprise. "He's going to be here in five minutes," she said. "The doorman promised to delay him for a couple of minutes." She saw Margaret and Paul, Carolyn Sue and De Vere, and a lot of others she didn't recognize. Which one was Lorna? Probably the sleek, glamorous woman with red-gold hair and the carriage of a model. She caught a glimpse of Roberta in red, looking daggers at the woman, but she held Rich Centner's arm tightly.

Lucy dashed to the terrace, and found that everything was arranged perfectly. The lights glowed in the dusk, and several silver Mylar balloons floated among the pots of flowers and the little trees. The white-jacketed bartender was already serving drinks. She could smell the barbecue in the warming tray on one of the tables. Mrs. Frost and Carlotta, both in black with white aprons, hovered, straightening piles of plates and baskets of forks and knives. It was going to be perfect.

She figured she had only about two minutes to get into her sexy gold dress. It was a breathless two minutes, but she managed to emerge from her room, dressed, combed, and made up just as the door opened and Dale appeared.

"Surprise!" Everyone saw him at the same moment and shouted, then they all crowded around him. Dale looked stunned, then pleased. Roberta managed to detach herself from Centner and hugged her husband. Suddenly Dale caught Lucy's eye and he smiled. He seemed to know that she'd been responsible for the surprise.

He mouthed the words "thank you," and then was swept away by his guests. Lucy mingled.

Roberta said, "I suppose you're pretty pleased with

yourself. I wouldn't have thought to invite Lorna Hutchison myself."

"I don't know her," Lucy said. "Which one is she?"

"That strumpet over there talking to Susan. I couldn't believe she'd dare to show up."

"He is her father," Lucy said. "Well, it seems to have worked out."

"Where did you two go this afternoon?"

"Just around." She felt a little nervous thrill remembering what Dale was going to tell Roberta tonight.

Now the guests crowded around the food tables, filling their plates and having a grand old time. Except for Susan, who glared at Lucy every time she looked at her, and Greg, who had also shown up, to Lucy's surprise. The waiters were pouring champagne for a toast, and it was Greg who tapped on a glass to silence the chatter.

"As the son of the family," he said, "I take it upon myself to offer a birthday toast to my father. He's been a good father to Susan and me, and we expect to celebrate many more of his birthdays in the years to come. To Dad!"

They drank, they applauded, and Dale silenced them with a wave of his hand.

"This is a wonderful surprise," he said. "And I think I know who to thank for it." Roberta ducked her head shyly. Dale went on, "I've been lucky enough to have a wonderful person in my life, and she's made me very happy." Now it was Lorna's turn to look shy and a bit embarrassed. But it was Lucy who was smiling and watching him adoringly.

"Don't behave like a fool," Susan hissed from behind Lucy's back. "He wouldn't dare be talking about you."

"Maybe he is," Lucy said.

"Then it's a terrible insult to my mother."

Lucy shrugged it away.

"I have a small announcement I'd like to make on this happy occasion," Dale said. "And that is, I've decided that at this important milestone in my life, I am going to move in a new direction, and I expect that I will be spending my next fifty years with that wonderful person, Lucia Rose Grant."

Margaret clutched De Vere's arm and Carolyn Sue clutched Paul's. Roberta staggered back into the comforting arms of Audrey Cheever. Rich Centner had retreated to a distant corner of the terrace, as if to show he wasn't involved in any of this. Susan turned to Lucy and slapped her very hard across the face. Lorna wailed and sank to the ground.

Dale held out his hand to Lucy, and she went to him.

"I didn't think you'd tell her in quite this way," she said, "but it sure was dramatic."

The guests began to mill about, discussing the unexpected announcement in low voices. Roberta was leaning against the wall, white-faced and breathing heavily. Lucy dared to go to her.

"Roberta, it wasn't supposed to happen this way at all."

"Get out of my sight," Roberta managed to say, and suddenly all the ladies surrounded them, expressing deep sympathy and concern for her. Lucy they ignored pointedly.

"I won't let him go," Roberta was saying. "Not now, not ever." Dale came to her, but Roberta cringed at his touch.

"It had to be this way, Roberta."

"I will not let you go," Roberta said. "I gave you all the

freedom you wanted, I never complained about Lorna, but I will not surrender you to that . . . that lying child."

Margaret said to De Vere, "Poor Lucy. I doubt that she planned this as part of her surprise. Still, you have to give Dale credit for something."

"Very poor taste," Carolyn Sue said.

"How will it end?" Paul asked.

"Judging from what has happened so far," Margaret said, "very badly. What could Dale have been thinking?"

No one had a chance to speculate on what Dale Reeves' thoughts might have been, because Mrs. Frost and the waiters were just wheeling the huge birthday cake out onto the terrace. The candles were ablaze, and there was an elaborate arrangement of sparklers on the top layer, shooting flecks of silver into the air. Everyone moved toward the cake to admire it.

Everyone except the person whose scream ripped through the night.

In the ensuing confusion, Susan was the first to reach the terrace railing, then she was joined by Dale, and they both looked down.

"Oh no! Someone's fallen! I can see the body." People crowded around, looking, pointing, exclaiming. De Vere had disappeared, no doubt to summon help.

Margaret knew that someone was dead. She tried to remember what she had seen just before the scream and just after. Just people. She'd noticed the golden gleam of Lucy's dress somewhere in the crowd that was moving toward the cake. She was handing Dale one of the silver balloons.

If only Margaret knew who had fallen. The wall around the terrace was reasonably high. No one could have accidentally fallen over it. A person would have to climb up on it to jump, or be pulled up and then pushed. Margaret didn't like the idea of murder once again intruding on her life, but there were certainly enough bad feelings around to make it possible. And there was enough distress to make suicide a possibility.

"He didn't even get to cut the cake," Carolyn Sue said. "Well, at least it wasn't Dale who fell. He's right over there with De Vere."

"But where's Lucy," Margaret asked. "I don't see her anywhere."

"And Roberta's missing, too," Carolyn Sue said.

Roberta wasn't missing for long. She was found lying on a fashionable street off Park Avenue, right below her apartment, battered by the fall, instantly dead on impact.

Dale made the announcement to his guests, who spoke to the police and then were allowed to leave. No one had seen anything, not Roberta on the edge of the terrace, no one near her, nothing.

"Suicide, if you ask me," Audrey Cheever said, although no one had asked her. "After that performance that Dale put on, she couldn't face living anymore."

"Definitely murder," someone else said. "I heard her say she'd never let Dale go, and that cutie of his probably heard her say it as well. Those Texas people are not to be trifled with."

Margaret watched the Mylar balloon disappear into the night until it was just a tiny speck of silver among the stars.

Roberta was a tall woman of some substance. She was also not stupid, so the only way she could have gotten atop the parapet was with the aid of someone stronger than she. Lucy was not that person, at least she hoped not.

After a while, Lucy crept out of her room, to which she

had retreated, no longer wearing her gold dress but dark slacks and a T-shirt.

She looked at Dale surrounded by police and went to find Margaret.

"This is the worst thing that's ever happened to me," she said. "Just when I was so happy. Then Roberta had to go and kill herself. I guess Dale and I are to blame."

"They haven't determined what happened," Margaret said. "I agree it was pretty brutal of Dale to break the news publicly that way, but it would have been just as painful for Roberta if he'd done it privately. I suppose you do share a bit of the blame, but it's mostly Dale's burden. Look, he's signaling to you."

"I don't think I want to talk to him now."

"He made a big commitment to you, Lucy. Remember, 'for better or worse.' "

"Okay," she said.

"Wait, Lucy. I wanted to ask you. I saw you handing a balloon to Dale just before the cake came out."

"He didn't want to take it," she said, "but I tied the ribbon around his wrist. It was just a kind of joke."

"What happened to it? The balloon, I mean."

Lucy shrugged. "I guess it got loose somehow and floated away."

Margaret saw that De Vere was still talking earnestly to Dale, while a few remaining guests hovered nearby, waiting their turn. She knew De Vere hated it when she interfered, but she had to do it.

"Sam, could I interrupt?"

His look said, No, you may not, but his voice said, "What is it?"

"I wanted to tell Dale how sorry I am about what happened." She stretched out her hands to him in a comforting gesture. Dale reached out and took her hands in his. There it was, a broken piece of ribbon around his wrist.

"Sam, I've got to talk to you privately. Right now."

De Vere opened his eyes in surprise at her tone, but he took her arm and walked a few steps away from Dale.

"Did your people find anything but the body down there?"

"Like what?"

"One of the balloons."

"As a matter of fact, Mrs. Reeves was holding the string of one of those silver balloons when they looked at the body."

"Look at Dale Reeves' wrist. He's got a broken piece of the string they used for the balloons on it. I saw Lucy tie a balloon on him as a joke." Margaret took a deep breath and went on. "Sam, he knows what happened. He knows whether she jumped and grabbed the balloon's string as she was falling, or else he knows that he pushed her and she held on to the balloon and tore the ribbon when she went over the side."

"Margaret, I've told you a hundred times that I don't want you mixed up in murder." But he went quickly to Dale and handled the matter of the string as evidence. The two men were talking again, and Dale didn't look very happy.

"He said she jumped," De Vere told Margaret later. "Someone would have seen her resisting him if he tried to push her."

"Everyone was rushing to look at the cake. There was nobody to see anything at the edge of the terrace. And maybe she didn't resist all that much. He didn't leave her much to live for, but he had a motive, after all. Here he's proclaimed his love for another woman, but his wife told a lot of people that she'd never let him go. So he may have decided to create a permanent separation."

"We may be able to tell the way she fell from the way she landed. It's going to be hard to prove he did it."

Lucy approached De Vere timidly. "I know I'm to blame for what happened," she said. "Roberta never would have died if I hadn't come into Dale's life. Can I talk to him for a minute?"

"Go ahead," De Vere said. He kept his eye on her as she walked toward Dale. "That kid is going to carry a lot of guilt for a long time."

Margaret watched Lucy hand Dale a small, gaily wrapped package. He smiled faintly, and opened it. Then he hugged her, and she came back to Margaret and De Vere.

"His birthday present," she said. "It's one of those pretty colored tree frogs that live in the rain forest, made out of plastic. I told him that they're becoming extinct, and you know what he said? He said, 'Some things have to die. Roberta had to die. I didn't want to do it, but she wasn't going to let me be with you.'"

Lucy burst into tears, and Margaret watched De Vere and his colleagues take away the distinguished dentist to the stars.

Carolyn Sue was still hanging about. She said, "Cheer up, Lucia Rose. We're goin' home to Dallas until this is just a bad dream. My momma always used to say that living well is the best revenge, but however she died, Roberta turned that sayin' right around, and got her revenge by dyin'."